THE CHRISTMAS SNEAK

HOPE'S TURN HOLIDAYS

MARIE HARTE

NO BOX BOOKS

THE CHRISTMAS SNEAK
Hope's Turn Holidays

Ex-NFL star Deacon Flashman had the perfect woman in the palm of his hands…and dropped the ball.

Considering his past performances, that isn't news. An injury cut short his football career, and then he got taken for millions by a greedy ex-wife. But Deacon's luck has changed. With the holidays close, he's getting a second chance. Nora Nielson, the woman who got away, is back. Now he needs to figure out how to get into her good graces. A relationship with Nora is everything he wants…and everything that scares him. But to let the past go, he'll have to go big or go home. And the stakes have never been higher.

THE CHRISTMAS SNEAK
Copyright © December 2019 by Marie Harte
ISBN 9781642920444
No Box Books
Cover by Sweet 'N Spicy Designs
Edited by Stefanie Carol

For exclusive excerpts, news, and contests, sign up for **Marie's newsletter**. http://bit.ly/MHnewsltr

ACKNOWLEDGMENTS

To all the readers who asked about Deacon's story, this book would not have been written without you. And to my incredible friend and editor, Stef, you always come through in a pinch. Many, many thanks.

CHAPTER 1

Hope's Turn, Oregon
November

Outside, the weather had dipped several degrees. A fireplace burned in the living room, making the area toasty. But it was the woman practically in his lap making Deacon overly warm.

And not in a good way.

"You are so hot." Meghan ran her hands over Deacon's sweater, kissing her way along his throat. "I haven't seen you in forever, baby."

It had been a few weeks ago, and he'd only stopped by then because he'd felt guilty he'd been avoiding her.

She purred. "You're sexy and rich and all mine."

Finally, she'd said out loud what he'd been suspecting since the beginning. She'd called him hot? Deacon felt nothing but cold.

"Maybe we could spend our Thanksgiving in Maui, baby. Think about it."

The stunning redhead had turned from an attractive possibility to a definite flag on the play after the first time she'd mentioned his perceived wealth. But Deacon knew he was overly sensitive about money. Just because his ex-wife had been a gold-digging user didn't mean every woman was out to con him. He'd wanted to prove to himself that he could give anyone a second chance. But a third? No way.

"Deacon?" Meghan pulled back, sensing his lack of interest, apparently. "Are you okay?"

They'd met two months ago at a friend's anniversary party. He'd tried to play it cool, but she'd been all over him from the first, quick to jump into bed and give him anything he wanted. To be honest, Deacon was used to women who catered to him, adored him, and made him feel special. He'd had looks and brawn before joining the NFL. And life as a professional athlete had been like rolling out the red carpet on his dating life. Despite all that, he'd never had an ego, he didn't think.

Probably why Rhonda had been able to step all over him.

And there was that one particular woman who didn't seem to like him much. One he thought about at odd times for no apparent reason.

Nora Freakin' Nielson.

God, stop thinking about her.

He pushed her sardonic wit and sexy smirk to the back of his mind as he tried to figure out how to get out of spending the holiday with *this* woman after his body and his money, and not necessarily in that order. Though he didn't want to hurt Meghan's feelings, he'd reached his breaking point.

He pasted a smile on his face. "No way I'm going to Maui. I need to get right back to work after Thanksgiving."

Meghan's full lips turned down in a pout. It wasn't a good look, though she seemed to use it a lot when not getting her way. *Damn.* Eight weeks with her had been eight weeks too many. Why the hell had he agreed to spend the holiday with her? Oh right, because Nora would be attending this year's family Thanksgiving.

"But Deacon, we need to spend time together," Meghan whined. "I haven't seen you in forever. Let's take the time, just you and me."

"Um, I thought you said your folks were coming into town."

"Plans changed. I wanted to spend my holiday with you, and I knew you wouldn't come if you thought I'd put you before my parents. I'll visit with them at Christmas. What do you say? You should come with me to meet them." Her eyes shone with enthusiasm. "Just us on a private jet to Seattle, then maybe we can fly to Alaska for New Year's if you don't want Maui. Or take a cruise to Europe?" Her eyes brightened. "That would be fun."

"Meghan, I can't take that much time off."

"Sure you can. You're the boss."

"I *co-own* the brewery. We're not that big yet, and in any case, I'm not rolling around in money." *Not like I used to be...*

Her eyes turned hard. "What? I'm not worth spending a few dollars on?" She leaned forward, her décolletage enticing...and... well...boobytrapped.

No pun intended.

He muffled immature laughter she would *not* appreciate. "Look. Clearly this isn't working. You want a sugar daddy. Meghan, that's not me."

She frowned. "That's not true. Deacon, I like you a lot."

My wallet, you mean. He extricated himself from her hold and left the couch. "I like you too. I think you're sweet. But we want different things."

"That's bull. You want me. Hell, you wanted me the last time we were together. More than once, if you remember," she snapped. "Oh, I see. You want sex, so you come over to my place. But when I want a real relationship, you decide I'm not good enough for you and your damn millions?"

He sighed. He should have ended things a few days after meeting her. But he'd hoped they might have more. An image of Nora shaking her head at him popped into his mind's eye, and he silently swore as he pushed her behind yet another mental door. "Let's be honest. You came on to me that first night. I politely said no *three times*. Then, well, you're gorgeous. I figured if you wanted me that much, I should see where things went."

She turned scarlet but didn't disagree.

"Meghan, we've had fun. But you seem determined to get me to buy you airfare, diamonds" —she'd brought that up on their last date— "or something to show you I care. With me, a relationship should be about more than money." He'd taken her out for dinner and fun, and he'd always paid. But lately he'd seen the truth about what she really wanted. *Been there, done that.*

"Obviously." She sniffed, working up a tear maybe? "But you have me all wrong. I don't just care about your bank account. I like... I think I might love you, Deacon." Tears welled.

"I wish I could believe that." He hated to be a hard-ass, but he'd been played the fool before. "Unfortunately, I don't."

Her eyes narrowed, the hint of waterworks gone. "Fine. Then screw you. Get out. I don't need you. I can get any man I want." She sneered. "You think some has-been NFL star is top of the food chain in this town? Think again."

"I wish you the best, Meghan." He grabbed his coat and didn't look back, even when she threw a shoe at the wall and wailed his name.

God, what had he been doing with her? *Has-been NFL star?* Yep, that was Deacon's life now. The glory days in the past, his life one big do-over. More tired than he'd been in a long time, he went straight to bed the moment he arrived home.

The next morning, his cell phone rang and rang, waking him. He blearily glanced at his phone, then looked through and listened to his messages. The last few calls and texts had been from Meghan, alternately cursing him out and begging him to come back. He started to put his phone on mute but saw his brother's caller ID when the phone rang again.

"Mitch?" he answered.

"It's time! Get your ass to the hospital. Hurry." Mitch disconnected.

Deacon's brain caught up with his brother's words. It was finally happening. Deacon was about to become an uncle for the second time in a year, though this kid would be brand spankin' new and not a sarcastic teenager.

Excitement filled him. He hurried to dress. He needed to be there for his brother, sister-in-law, and nephew. He couldn't wait!

And if he took a little extra care with his appearance, it had nothing to do with the sexy—no, *obstinate*—woman who'd also be waiting for the baby's birth. Nora could sneer and snark at him as much as she wanted to. Hell, truth be told, he looked forward to it.

With a grin, he raced to the hospital, and this time he allowed thoughts of the fiery beauty to linger while he remembered how much he wished he could forget her.

St. Mary's Hospital

"WHY IS THIS TAKING SO LONG?" *THAT MAN* GRIPED FOR THE FIFTH TIME in as many minutes.

Nora forced herself to take a moment before responding. A glance around the hospital waiting room showed a group of people assembled to celebrate a monumental event. They'd gathered together with love, anticipation making them giddy, excitable, and—she eyed the giant with the attitude—irritable.

This was Becca's day, or rather, Becca's *baby's* day, as the precious little girl readied to greet the world. Dubbed "the Christmas baby," though they technically had another month until Santa came to visit, Baby Flashman would be loved by her parents, half-brother, and bevy of relatives eager to meet the newest addition to the brood.

Though cousins, Becca and Nora were more like sisters. Nora couldn't have had a better best friend. Becca deserved every happiness; her lovely husband did too. Nora loved Mitch.

She just wished he'd been born an only child.

As if sensing her regard, Deacon Flashman, Mitch's older, obnoxious brother, met her gaze. His left brow rose in question. If he wasn't taller than Sasquatch, she'd sock him in the eye just to see if he'd lose that aggravating expression of superiority.

Instead, she smiled. "Well, Deacon, maybe you could go in there and give Becca tips on how to pass something the size of a bowling ball out of her lady shoot."

"*Nora.*" Nora's mother sounded shocked, though she shouldn't have been. She did know her daughter, after all. "Be nice." *Be nice*—a phrase Nora had been hearing for thirty-four plus years.

Her father, standing close by, laughed, as did Deacon's parents.

Deacon grimaced. "Oh, er. I'm happy to wait out here."

"No, really. Let's talk about the biology of birthing a child."

Her nephew tugged her by the arm and leaned closer to whisper, "You're showing a lot of teeth, Aunt Nora. Let's get something to eat. I'm hungry."

"You're always hungry."

"Yep." Simon nodded. "Feed me."

She let the super tall teenager lead her toward the elevators. "He's insufferable."

"Uh-huh." Simon looked down at her with his mother's hazel eyes. He had his father's sandy hair and good looks, but he was Becca's boy down to the bone. Sarcastic and smart and quite the athlete. When his father had died, Simon and his mom had grieved. So this second chance at a rounded family was more than welcome.

They entered the elevator and rode to the cafeteria on the third floor.

"Sorry." She wasn't, exactly. But she didn't want to ruin it for Simon. After all, one didn't get a little sister every day. It wasn't Simon's fault Deacon rubbed her the wrong way. Once, she'd thought things might be different between them. But no, he'd proven he was just like all the rest. A mistake.

They left the elevator and headed for the a la carte line.

Simon glanced at her once before honing back in on the food. "You know, when I apologize like that, with all that fake sincerity, Mom just looks at me. Like this." He gave her the old I-don't-believe-you stare Becca had perfected before adding a few plates of food to his tray.

"Fine. I'm so, so *s-o-r-r-y*," she dragged out.

He rolled his eyes.

After grabbing a doughnut and coffee, she paid and sat with him at a nearby table. "Are you excited about meeting your sister?" She picked at her treat but lingered over the coffee, which tasted surprisingly good.

Simon shoveled food into his growing body while managing a grin. "Yep. Mom and Mitch said I'll have to help with diapers. Not so sure about that, but it'll be fun to have someone else to blame when things go wrong."

She laughed. "Uh-huh. Might have to wait until she's a little older for that."

"I'm going to teach her how to throw a touchdown pass." Simon's passion revolved around sports, in particular, football.

"I think between you and Mitch, she'll be the first female running back in the NFL."

"She can follow in my footsteps."

"Big dreams, little guy." At the face he made, she chuckled. "So how is life with the ex-football star? Still amazing, or has it become normal now?" Mitch had come to live in Hope's Turn a little over a year ago after retiring from the NFL at the top of his game. He had a ton of money, two Superbowl rings, owned a huge house in the mountains, and helped coach Simon's high school football team when not organizing free sports opportunities for the kids in town.

He treated Becca like she could do no wrong. For that alone Nora would have loved him. But he'd also accepted Simon into his life without issue and treated him like his son.

She wished he had a clone she could marry. Unfortunately, the closest thing to his DNA came in the form of Dick—er, Deacon—Flashman.

"Life is great. We're all happy. Mom's thrilled. Mitch is awesome." Simon's voice hitched.

Nora stared at him in concern. "Simon?"

He let out a slow, wavery breath. "Sorry. It's just... I'm so happy. Everything's so good lately. I'm worried something bad will happen. Like with Dad." A terrible car accident had taken Simon's father eight years ago.

She put her hand over his on the table. "What happened to your dad was a fluke. You can't predict those kinds of things. Let yourself be happy when life is good."

"And make lemonade when life gives you lemons?" he added drily, sounding better.

"Heck no. Make limoncello. Lemonade is for wusses."

He laughed, looking less stressed.

They chatted about school and his girlfriend, who would be arriving just as soon as she could. With the Thanksgiving holiday upon them, the baby had come at a less than convenient time for turkey lovers. Not that Nora had made other plans. This year the entire family had planned to celebrate together at Mitch's house. His parents, Nora's folks—who were as much Becca's parents as Nora's—Nora, and Simon.

Fortunately, Deacon had made other plans in town.

Everyone had wanted to stay close, anticipating Becca's labor.

Nora wondered what it must be like to have a man who loved you wholeheartedly. How it felt to hold your baby in your arms. Sometimes she envied Becca. And then she'd hate herself for feeling anything but glad for her cousin. Becca had lost the love of her life when Simon was just a young boy.

It had taken her a while to recover, and for the past eight years she'd been living a half-life, devoted to motherhood but lacking any intimate bonds for herself. Her world had revolved around work and her small family, of which Nora felt privileged to be a part. Now Becca had a husband, an amazing son, and a new baby to light up her world.

So unlike Nora, who felt alone even when surrounded by a crowd. She wondered if the invisible "Desperate and Available" sign around her neck was responsible for her lack of worthwhile offers. Her last date had claimed he loved her and wanted to move in, no doubt rent free, following their first *and only* dinner together.

She sighed.

"Are you going to eat that?" Simon asked, pointing at her remaining doughnut.

She pushed it toward him. "No, go ahead."

She watched him eat, remembering back when she could stuff herself on chips and sweets and not pay for it on the scale. "Are you upset you guys didn't make the playoffs this year? I mean, you played varsity as a sophomore. That's a big deal. Too bad the football team couldn't carry Riverdown High further."

"It's okay we didn't make playoffs. It's a growing year, and Deacon said I should be prepared for college scouts my last two seasons at school. I've got time."

"Not much." She looked at him, feeling the minutes tick by. "I can't believe you're already in high school. I still remember the first time I held you, and you peed all over me."

Simon flushed. "Come on, Nora. I was a baby. Do you have to keep bringing that up?"

She smirked. "Oh, yeah. Until you're at least forty."

He glared. "Well then, I guess I'll have to share some of your embarrassing stories."

"Oh please. My life is an open book." In a lower voice, she added, "Probably why I'm dateless at thirty-four."

"Thirty-five, you mean."

She poked Simon in the shoulder. "Not quite. My birthday is a while away."

"Um, isn't it in on Christmas Eve?"

"Well, technically. I—"

Her father rushed toward them, his face wreathed in joy. "The baby's here! It's a girl, six pounds, eight ounces. Becca's just fine."

Nora's vision blurred, and she wiped her cheek. "Oh man, I'm an aunt again!" She hugged Simon, who let out a loud whoop.

Self-pity, denial, and loneliness could wait. She had a niece to cuddle and a best friend to hug. Stat.

CHAPTER 2

*S*everal hours later, Deacon stared at the pink, wrinkled blessing in his brother's arms and grinned. "Man, she's so soft and mushed. Looks just like you."

Mitch chuckled. "Ass." He kissed his daughter on the forehead. "Want to hold her?"

"Me?" Deacon had watched everyone fuss over the proud parents and baby, waiting impatiently for his turn. He'd never held a newborn before. Sadly, his time with Rhonda hadn't produced anything but animosity and heartache. But this... Man, Mitch had outdone himself. "You did good, Bro."

Mitch smiled. "I know."

Deacon chuckled. "Okay, gimme." He carefully held the little girl all wrapped up in a soft blue blanket, conscious of her frailty. "Man, she's barely heavier than a ball. But don't worry. I know not to throw her."

Mitch sighed. "Not instilling any confidence here, moron."

Deacon ignored him, in love with his brand-new niece. "What's her name? Come on, tell me."

Mitch glanced around. "Okay, but don't let on that you know. We're supposed to make an official announcement to everyone at the same time." He paused. "We've named her Ava Honoria Flashman. Ava after Grandma."

"And Honoria?"

"Hello. After her aunt? You know. Nora."

Deacon felt a wicked grin break out. "Nora's name is actually Honoria?"

"Crap. Forget I mentioned it." But Mitch's sly expression said he didn't mean it. "At least hold onto the name until we let everyone know. Then use it to your heart's content."

And he would. Deacon had been bothered by Nora Nielsen for as long as he'd known her. Attracted, annoyed, and baffled. His relationship with the clever woman had gone from friendly and most definitely attracted to a man brushed aside, though he should have expected it. He still wondered if he'd made the right decision by avoiding her following their one and only date.

Nah, he'd been smart to dodge her. Considering even her snappish comebacks made him want to go caveman and drag her off to the nearest cave/bed/closet for some close-up and personal time, he knew it had been best to keep out of her way.

"Mom's been pretty good about not being all over you guys," he commented.

"Yeah, though she's been super excited about being a grandma." Mitch pursed his lips. "Well, actually, Simon gets the privilege of being the first grandkid. He was bragging about it when he met Ava for the first time, so of course Mom and Dad made sure he knows how special he is to them too. Then he winked at me. The conniver."

"I love that kid." Deacon chuckled. "He knows how to take advantage of doting old people. And if you tell Mom I called her old, I'll deny it, so don't bother."

Mitch chuckled and shot Deacon a side-glance. After a pause, he said, "You were supposed to go first having babies, you know."

"Imagine how awful that would have been with Rhonda. She'd hold a kid over my head for every damn thing."

Mitch nodded. "That's a good point. You're so much better off without her."

Deacon knew that. Still didn't help him in the dark of night, when he stared at the ceiling of his bedroom, all alone, riddled with his inadequacies. *And man, am I a candidate for throwing the best pity-party of the decade.* He shrugged off the negativity that didn't belong here, in this place, and focused on the joy in his arms.

After some quiet time holding Ava, he cleared his throat, trying best to phrase what he wanted to know. "So, uh, Nora."

"What about her?" Mitch watched him, but Deacon didn't trust the innocent look in his brother's eyes.

"She's still a major pain in the ass. Got all sarcastic when I was bitching about how long it was taking for the kid to pop out."

"I can't blame you. I was kind of freaked out about it too. Sixteen hours in labor. Poor Becca, yet she looks like she's glowing." Mitch wore a dopey grin. "She's my world, man."

A twinge of envy hit Deacon before he shrugged it away. "Like I said, you did good."

Mitch's smile widened.

Deacon sighed. "You're going to be super cheery for a long, long time, aren't you?"

"Yep."

"Just…tone down that happy crap in the mornings, okay?"

"Maybe. But it'll cost you." Mitch reached out, and Deacon deposited the baby in his arms.

"I'm prepared to pay." Not a morning person, Deacon usually warmed up to tolerable by ten, maybe eleven if he didn't have coffee to jolt him back to humanity.

"Tell me again why you couldn't make it to our originally scheduled Thanksgiving dinner. We had everybody here for once. Except you."

Deacon had never mentioned his first and only date with Nora. But his brother had picked up on the tension between them. As had Becca and Simon. Fortunately, he and Nora had done their best to avoid each other for months. And everyone had been too polite or distracted to say anything over the holiday, what with the baby coming.

"I was planning to spend the time with my girlfriend. Unfortunately, we hit a rough patch."

Mitch's brows rose. "Sandra?"

"Meghan." Deacon shrugged. "She's now my ex-girlfriend, along with Sandra."

"And Rachel, and Sue, and Michelle…" Mitch shook his head while he cradled his daughter and made gooey faces at her. "Hear that, Ava? Uncle Deacon bit the dust again."

"*I* called it off, moron."

Mitch gave him a pitying look. "Bro, you need to relax with all the women. Meghan is like the eighth woman you've dated and broken up with in the past two weeks."

"You're exaggerating."

Mitch just looked at him.

Deacon flushed. "She and I dated for the two months, you know. It's just… Look, leaving the game was tough. But hey, injuries happen. Then Rhonda sucker punched me and took everything. It took a while for me to get my feet under me."

"A good two years and change," Mitch muttered. "I sincerely hope karma bites Rhonda's big ass."

Deacon appreciated the sentiment. "We both know I wasn't in a good place." Deacon hated remembering how close he'd come to just saying to hell with it all and ending things. For good. "It makes sense I was gun-shy to date again. I was kind of freaked out by it."

"Yeah, because all the sexy women in town fawning all over you is scary."

Deacon felt his face heat. "Shut up. Women *are* scary."

Mitch smirked. "Especially Nora."

"*Anyway*" —no way was Deacon touching that one— "At first, dating again was unsettling. Then I started having fun. Getting to know women, not being in the spotlight anymore, being a regular guy, it felt good."

"I hate to break it to you, but you're a lot less than normal." Mitch looked him over, from head to toe. "First of all, you're six-four and still built like a linebacker."

"Hey, I was a quarterback." Deacon scowled.

"And a big QB at that." Mitch grinned at the finger Deacon shot him. "But everyone in town knows you spent a solid seven years in the NFL. They might not know the state of your finances, but they know you were big league. And now you co-own a brewery. The notion that you have money has to be there."

"I know. I just wish I was as rich as everyone thinks I am."

Mitch frowned. "Do you need money? Becca and I have plenty to—"

"*No.*" Deacon lowered his voice when the baby stirred. "No, Midas, I do not. I'm actually pretty good right now." Rhonda had taken him for everything she could get, leaving a once-million-dollar star athlete at a mid-six figure reality. Not such a hardship, except he'd also been stuck with her debts, taking on a lot more he couldn't afford to lose.

Mitch and his parents had offered Deacon help, but he'd been too proud to accept a handout, ashamed at how he'd gone from hero to zero thanks to a torn rotator cuff ending his career and a greedy wife ending his shot at a happily-ever-after.

Then a lifeline in the form of Roy Thompson, his best friend, had given Deacon purpose.

Now he co-owned a successful brewpub with expansion on the horizon. But it had taken nearly all his savings to get the brewery where it needed to be. With Roy's knowledge and contacts, along with Deacon's money and networking, they had finally started to show a major profit, allowing Deacon to take a paycheck again.

"Good to know you're not broke," Mitch said. "Then maybe you'll be hosting our next major holiday after Christmas?"

"Please. No one can compete with your mansion in the mountains." Deacon scoffed. "My tiny bungalow is way too small for family."

"You're such a liar. Bungalow? More like a mini-mansion of your own in town."

"My house is maybe a third the size of yours."

Mitch raised a brow. "Whatever. Your place still ain't small. Be honest. You have plenty of space in that home of yours. You just choose to keep it a bachelor pad."

"Yep. Complete with bras and thongs all over the place," Deacon deadpanned. "Your house has an indoor pool, media room, and a state-of-the-art weight room. That's in addition to all the other crap you have. Dude, a reading room? You have enough space to designate rooms for reading and games. And movies! My place can't compete with that."

Mitch also had the most important thing of all, something Deacon sorely wanted but didn't think he'd ever have.

A family.

After a moment, Mitch asked, "Has Nora seen it?"

"No. I—what?" That had come out of nowhere.

"I just think it's interesting that you and Nora seemed pretty tight at the beginning of the year. And then it's like you two are barely ever in the same room together. If you are, you're either ignoring each other or snapping at each other."

"We don't get along." But he sure wished they did. Lately, whenever out with a woman, Deacon mentally compared her to Nora. Inevitably, his date would come up lacking.

"Uh-huh." Mitch watched him. "So why did you and Sandra—sorry, Meghan—break up?"

"She was a little too interested in my finances. Rhonda started out like that."

"You probably made a good call to end things. But do you ever wonder if maybe everyone you date is going to come up short? You got hammered by your ex. It's only natural you—"

"Don't want to talk about it anymore." Deacon forced a smile. "Let's just enjoy the baby and your family. Okay?"

Mitch's face softened. "Okay, Deac. Then, since you're obviously not doing Thanksgiving with your new lady, maybe you can help Mom and Dad do it at our place in a few days."

"You sure you want everyone there with a new baby?"

"Yeah." Mitch's eyes started to shine, and his voice sounded gruff when he said, "Family is everything, man."

Deacon pulled him in for a gentle hug, careful not to smush Ava. "I feel you. And I swear I'll be nice to Nora. Just for you."

"Aw, now I really feel bad for pantsing you in fifth grade."

"Still *such* an ass." Deacon pulled back. "Fatherhood hasn't made a difference, has it?"

Mitch snickered. "Nope. Not a bit. Just remember this conversation when you're expecting your own."

CHAPTER 3

*N*ora didn't know what she'd been thinking by offering to help with late Thanksgiving this year. It should have been Mitch and Becca's responsibility. Mitch was supposed to hire the best caterer for the meal, and Becca would handle dessert because she insisted only *she* could make a decent pumpkin pie. Becca still had a tough time accepting the fact she'd married a rich man. Just letting him cater the meal had been a huge deal.

But because of the baby, Mitch had been scattered and forgot to confirm the caterer, and the last thing on Becca's mind was pie. Mitch's parents had gladly stepped in. Then Nora's parents offered to help. Everything should have been taken care of, yet somehow, *Nora* had been volunteered to work alongside Deacon while they set the table and ran errands for the experts in the kitchen.

"I could cook," she muttered, wishing she'd gotten turkey detail instead of being relegated to resident fetch girl.

"I could totally cook," Deacon seconded, though from what Mitch had once said, the man could barely boil water. "Better than having to decorate every damn thing." He placed a ceramic pumpkin in the middle of the table.

"Where's Simon?" Her teenage buffer had disappeared over an hour ago, leaving her in awkward silences with Deacon.

"The slacker is using the sister excuse." Deacon frowned. "According to my mother, Simon needs bonding time with Ava, so he can't possibly help set the table, run errands for the grandparents, or take the dog out for walks."

Funny, because Nora could have sworn she'd seen the boy laughing with his girlfriend in the game room half an hour ago. But she was no narc. "Speaking of the dog, where is she? I haven't seen Oreo for a while."

"No idea, and I don't want to know. She's cute but a menace. I swear, that thing poops more than a herd of elephants, and on an hourly basis."

Nora tried to bite back a smile, but he saw it.

"Laugh it up until it's your turn. I'm telling you, that thirty-five pound dog craps fifty-pound loads."

"Gross. Stop." She bit her lip and turned away, fiddling with the glass-ware. Wow. They were having an actual conversation, and she hadn't gone for his throat yet. Perhaps the holiday had brought more than one miracle.

The silence settled between them once more.

They finished with place settings until Nora realized they were short one butter knife. She fetched it from the buffet and looked for anything else she might have missed.

"Deacon," his mother called.

With a sigh, Deacon left, only to return carrying a large platter of deviled eggs and an olive tray, both covered in plastic wrap. He set them on the buffet. Then he moved more chairs into the room around the extra-large dining table. She straightened the place settings, wondering how to break away without looking as if she were afraid of being in the same room with him. Which she totally wasn't.

Nora didn't fear Deacon. But she did fear saying or doing something to ruin the family fun. Babies, couples, together time. She should have been reveling in all the happiness. Instead, she wanted to run far from it all.

She stared at the table, her mind blanking before a familiar phrase came to mind that fit the occasion—*Bah, humbug.*

Muffling pathetic laughter at herself, she wondered what excuse to use to leave early. Feeling so out of sorts around everyone, Nora didn't want her odd mood to affect the others.

Deacon cleared his throat.

She glanced up to see him standing with his hands in his jean pockets, staring at her. She wished his navy sweater didn't make his eyes appear so dang blue. Looking into those dark peepers was like daring to swim in shark-infested waters. Nope. Time to find something else to occupy her. Just as she readied to make a break for the study, he spoke.

"So, ah, how's it feel to be an aunt again?"

Talking about kiddos seemed safe enough. Congenial, even. She forced a smile. "It's great. I already love Simon. The addition of Baby Ava's going to be a treat." Thinking about how beautiful Becca's baby was, this time when she smiled it came naturally. "I bet *she* won't throw a fit when she's older and I'm taking her clothes shopping."

"I take it Simon wasn't a fan of trying on pants a few weeks ago?" Deacon smirked. "I might have heard a thing or two about it at football practice."

"The kid's been wearing floods because he's growing so fast." She made a face. "I should have made Mitch take him, but I was trying to be nice. With Becca as big as a house and crabby, I thought I'd save them all some hassle and help my nephew get decent clothes for school. Man, was I wrong." She glanced at him. "Were you and Mitch a pain with your parents?"

"Not me." He gave a disingenuous smile. "Mitch was a handful. I was the good son."

His mother entered the dining room and snorted, apparently having overheard. "You wish. Mitch listened. Not you. Too cool to obey Mom until Dad walked in carrying his belt."

Nora studied the big man dwarfing his mom trying to act innocent. "Did your dad hit you?" She couldn't imagine quiet and kind Lee Flashman, the same man who had chastised Mitch for talking too harshly to the dog and who blushed when his wife called him cute, doing anything mean to his kids.

"No, but he threatened an awful lot. I didn't get this big until college, so it wasn't like I could take on the old man if he started swinging." Deacon grinned at his mom.

Brenda Flashman shook her head, her silver bangs ruffling. "Don't listen to him, Nora. Lee never raised a hand to our boys. Though plenty of times I wouldn't have been opposed. Fortunately, my boys were easy. Put Mitch in the corner and he lost his mind. Take Deacon away from sports practice and he was miserable and soon begging for mercy." Brenda sighed. "Ah, the good old days."

"Mom."

"Really?" Nora would love to see Deacon begging for anything.

He must have read her mind, because he chuckled. "Great, Mom. Now you have Nora out for my blood. Don't believe her," he said to Nora. "I only pretended to be afraid so they'd quit harping on me to clean my room." He mock-cringed when his mother neared. "I'm just teasing, Mom. Please. Don't beat me again. At least not in public."

"Really, Deacon. I know how not to leave a mark." Brenda winked at Nora. "Dealing with children all day long gave me the gift of tolerance —and a love of vodka." Brenda left, laughing.

Nora chuckled. She really liked the Flashmans. Brenda had a warm sincerity that immediately put one at ease. She corralled her grown sons and husband like a pro, the retired teacher in her apparent. And Nora could see where Deacon and Mitch had inherited their manly charm. Their father sounded gruff, but his eyes shone with pride, and he treated Becca and Simon with more than kindness. He'd accepted them right off, including Nora and her parents in his goodwill.

So why had Lee's oldest son turned into such a jerk?

She lifted a fork near her, seeing the silver glint under the lights, lost in thought.

When she'd first met Deacon, she'd done her best to hide a huge crush. He had to be the most attractive guy she'd ever seen. Not that he was classically good-looking; his features were too overpowering for that. But he had the tall, dark, and handsome thing going on. Hmm. More like tall, dark, and menacing—until he smiled. Deacon radiated kindness while wearing sarcasm like a second skin. He fascinated her on too many levels. So, she'd played it cool, pretending she hadn't noticed him checking her out and loving the fact he had.

Then they'd had that date that had gone nowhere...

"Why are you looking at me like you plan to stab me with the fork you're holding?"

She clutched the silverware tightly before setting it back next to the plate. She smoothed out the tablecloth and smiled at him through her teeth. "I'm going to see if they need anything else."

Did he seem relieved she was leaving his presence? She couldn't tell.

He gave her a bland smile back. "Sounds good. I'll go see if Mitch needs anything."

Unfortunately, Brenda needed another bag of stuffing mix. Nora's mother needed more whipping cream and a bag of apples for "a surprise and never you mind." Lee wouldn't mind more olives and snacks; he had a fondness for chips and cookies that his wife kept stealing, leaving him hankering. Mitch had decided they needed more dog food in case the storm that had been circling overhead hit earlier than expected, and would she mind taking Deacon with her so he could help her carry supplies? Heck, they might as well take Deacon's SUV since it had new tires and more room for everything.

So much for getting some freakin' space.

"You sure you're okay with me driving?" Deacon asked as he fiddled with the radio on their drive back into town.

They hadn't encountered much traffic coming down the mountain, though she was sure the crowds would pick up as the day waned, with people eager to hit the ski lodge for the weekend.

"Oh, sure. Fine."

"Fine." He repeated, a half smile on his face, and turned up the music.

Minutes passed.

They hadn't yet reached the grocery store when he shocked the heck out of her by apologizing. "Look, I'm sorry, okay?"

"Um…" She paused. "For what, exactly?"

He scowled at her before concentrating once more on the road. "For the awkwardness between us."

Nora refused to accept his remorse. *Yep, that's me. Graceless.* "Oh? I hadn't realized there was anything wrong with the way we deal with each other."

He gripped the wheel tighter. "Gimme a break. When we first met, we laughed and got along. Now, I can barely be in the same room with you before you're sniping at me for something."

She raised a brow and said nothing.

"I mean, so we had one date. I thought it went well. Then you started acting funny. You ignored my texts and got weird anytime we were in the same room together. And hell, you still act weird."

She blinked. "Excuse me?"

"You heard me." He sounded grim. "I think you're hot, and you're funny. I asked you out because I thought we might have something. Then you got all cold and never talked to me again."

"Oh my God. Seriously? Deacon, we dated once. It was a lot of fun. I agree. The next day you left on business and never talked to me again. Oh wait, you did…way back in February. You texted me that Becca needed me to pick up Simon from school. That was it."

"That's not true. First of all, I let you know I was leaving and that I'd call you when I got back." He shifted in his seat. "I called you more than once. Hell, we talk all the time."

"Are you being deliberately obtuse or are you just stupid?"

"Oh, that's nice."

"Seriously." She folded her arms over her chest to keep from reaching for his throat. "We had a great date. You made me laugh, and I was attracted. We had chemistry. Then you spazzed when you left, went out of town for a month—"

"Two weeks on business."

"—and came back with *a girlfriend.* You never answered my message about anything being wrong. You just came back to Hope's Turn with a significant other. Then you want to be friends and act like nothing's wrong?" Flabbergasted, she just looked at him. "Really? You ghosted me to my face, which shouldn't even be a thing."

"That's not how I remember it."

"Oh?" She turned in her seat to stare at his stubborn profile. "Do tell, Deacon. How *do* you remember it?"

DEACON FOCUSED ON THE ROAD, WISHING HE'D NEVER BROUGHT UP the subject. "I remember having a great time on our date. I never spazzed." Well, maybe. He could still remember how sweaty his palms had been and how his heart had raced when they'd come to the end of the date. How badly he'd wanted to kiss her, and how worried he'd been that he'd screw up a good thing. So, he'd left her with a smile and a promise to call again. "I did call you, you know. After our date. And not about picking up Simon."

"To tell me you were going out of town, which I already knew? Gee, thanks, Deac."

A glance at Nora showed her just as vibrant, beautiful, and sarcastic as always.

"I never ghosted you." The dating practice of simply fading away and ending communication instead of telling a date goodbye had always bothered him.

"No. You made it seem like we had the potential to have a relationship then came back to town with a woman on your arm as if we barely knew each other, no explanation whatsoever."

He huffed. "I think you're making too much of it. It's not like I was cheating on you with someone else. Damn, Nora. It was one dinner."

Yet it had been so much more than that. He'd found in Nora someone he liked and desired, and her impact had left him breathless. And anxious. He'd needed to slow things down, and then somehow, he'd met Michelle on the plane back to town and found in her someone who was fun, sexy, and not at all threatening.

Nora's reactions upon his return had been eye-opening, though. That passive-aggressive silent treatment she'd subjected him to had been something Rhonda would have pulled, reinforcing the notion he'd been right to take a break from the sexy brunette.

Nora glared at him and said something that sounded uncomplimentary under her breath. In a louder voice, she asked, "If you just wanted a platonic dinner date, why did you take me to a fancy restaurant and act like you liked me as more than a friend? Why act as if you wanted something more?"

He shrugged, unwilling to admit the truth to her when it still bothered *him* to think about it. "I wanted to take you somewhere nice. Not sure why that's such a bad thing."

She studied him. He could feel her gaze like a burn, trying to tear through his thick skin to see the heart of him. But she'd never get past the walls that kept his heart safe.

"You really are incredible, you know that?"

He eyed her before watching the road once more. "Well, thanks."

"That's not a compliment, dumbass."

He bit back a grin, preferring her anger to wounded silence. "I think you're pretty incredible too."

"I honestly have a hard time reconciling how you and Mitch can be related. He's so kind and handsome. And you're...you."

He ignored the familiar tinge of jealousy. He'd grown used to being the screwed up one in his family, so Nora's comments shouldn't hurt so much. "I'm the taller, bigger, better-looking Flashman, is that what you mean?"

She blew out a loud breath. "Yep, there's that ego again. I can't believe I ever went out with you."

They finally pulled into the grocery store parking lot. Thank God. He turned off the engine and swiveled to face her. "So why did you go out with me, then?"

"What?" She looked off balance.

"If I'm such a loser, why go out with me at all? For my money?" Where had that come from? He'd never thought that about her. At least, he hadn't been consciously aware of thinking it.

Nora didn't take offense, as he might have expected. Meghan sure the hell had when he'd asked her why she was so interested in his finances.

Nora laughed him off. "Money? I doubt you're better off than I am. You seemed nice, though. So I thought, why not?" She gave him a pitying smile that irritated the hell out of him. "Why not throw the sad brother a bone and accept his invite to dinner? You're not a bad looking guy." She looked him over and shrugged. "I guess."

"Uh-huh." Deacon might be a lot of things, but he knew his looks had always appealed to women. He might not be in the NFL anymore, but he continued to keep his body in top physical condition. That Nora was trying to convince him she might not like his looks was…interesting.

"Well, what can I say?" Nora shrugged. "I thought the date would go better than it did. And it didn't." Her expression didn't sit well with him, because she looked both disappointed and hurt. "But hey, you live, you learn."

"And what exactly did you learn?"

"That Becca and Mitch might have found something special, but you and I did *not*. Period. End of story." She shot him a bright smile. "Heck. It's the holidays. Let's put all that behind us. Sure, Deacon. I accept your apology. You don't need to keep avoiding family gatherings, and I'll try to be nicer, okay?"

"O-kay," he said slowly, not sure why her acceptance made him feel worse and not better. He'd screwed up again, apparently. And this time by trying to do the right thing. "So, friends?" He held out a hand.

She stared at him. A flash of something came and went in her eyes. "Sure." Her handshake was there and gone in an instant. Then she left the vehicle, talking at him with a pleasant if aloof smile. *At* him, not *to* him.

He sighed, wondering how he could keep doing the wrong thing around Nora when he only wanted things to be right.

CHAPTER 4

*D*eacon wished he'd never opened his stupid mouth in the car. Nora was acting fake, and he hated it.

From other people he expected platitudes or false compliments. But not from family. He much preferred Nora's condescension and teasing than this pretend-happy crap. But at least she was talking to him, so he did nothing to try to remedy the situation.

At the register, they waited while the clerk rang them up, and he noticed Nora sneak a candy bar onto the conveyor belt. The woman had a definite sweet tooth.

When she tried to pay for everything, he glared. "I got this."

"Gee, thanks, Deacon." Her thanks grated, because he couldn't tell if her appreciation was genuine.

"You're welcome," he growled and paid the cashier.

On the drive back, she sat staring out the window.

"Not eating your chocolate?"

She gave him a side glance before turning her attention back to the road. "It's for later."

Silence filled the small space, but having failed before, he was determined not to say the wrong thing again. He turned on the radio, and they listened to alternative rock as they drove back up the mountain. Dark clouds overhead turned the bright sunny day gray, and the large pines along the road swayed in the wind as the first snowfall trickled over the SUV.

"Let it snow," Nora muttered.

"If we're lucky, we'll just get a little bit. It's only supposed to be a few inches. The real heavy stuff should hold off for a few weeks from what I heard on the radio."

Deacon pulled into the long driveway which looped in front of the house. The stonework and natural foliage had been brightened with potted mums that had survived some unseasonably warmer weather for Central Oregon at this time of year. But with the oncoming storm, he didn't think they'd survive much longer.

A glance at Nora had him wondering if he'd survive…Thanksgiving.

He cleared his throat, and Nora glanced his way. "Do you ever wish you lived in a house this big?" He knew she lived on the same side of town as him, but he'd never been invited to her home. Or was it an apartment? He had no idea.

"It's nice, but it's too big for me." A strange look passed over her face. "I like my place."

"Did you buy or are you renting?"

"I'm renting. It's easier that way."

"Easier?"

"To get housing. Anymore, getting a home loan is no joke, especially if you're self-employed."

He nodded. "You edit for a few magazines, don't you?"

She shot him a sharp look. "I freelance edit for a few e-magazines and run social media content for some businesses in town."

"Nice. Lets you be your own boss."

"Yep." Her full lips quirked into a smile, captivating him with ease.

Hell, he'd noticed everything about her from day one. Sadly, his mind kept returning to how amazingly she filled out a bathing suit when they'd met at Mitch's for a pool party nearly a year ago. Nora had an average height, but she had curves in all the right places, every part of her in perfect proportion.

He loved her brown hair and brown eyes, features he'd overheard her complaining about as boring, yet Deacon always felt hard-pressed to look away from her.

"Something on my face?" she asked. "You're staring."

He hoped he didn't look as red as he felt. "Um, you had some fuzz on your hair, but it's gone now." *I am such an idiot.*

She ran a hand over her mink-dark hair, and his fingers itched to do the same.

Nora glanced at his mouth and frowned, her own cheeks turning pink.

The front door opened, and his mother poked her head out and waved. "Oh good. You're back!"

Nora rushed from the vehicle with a grocery bag in hand and disappeared inside. Deacon took a moment to compose himself before grabbing the rest. He dumped the groceries in the kitchen before darting away to check on Simon.

After a quick peek at the teenager and his girlfriend playing video games in the game room, Deacon escaped to a quiet area in the back of the house, where a fire had been lit and a bouquet of fall flowers decorated a table in the center of a room with a very tall ceiling, the walls lined with bookcases.

Deacon's brother, the book nerd, had always been into reading, mostly history and other dry nonfiction. Mitch had been happy to shelve Becca's novel collection with his own, Deacon could see, unless his brother had suddenly started reading mysteries and romances. Hell, with Mitch, who knew? The cozy room had floor-to-ceiling shelves complete with a rolling ladder, the kind that libraries and bookstores used. Or, you know, rich people with too much money to spend.

Deacon could only shake his head and stoke up the fire, sitting on a comfy sofa while he ignored words on paper and stared into the flames. Oreo trotted inside and jumped onto the couch she wasn't supposed to sit on.

"Are you allowed in here?"

Oreo sighed and curled up next to him. She put her muzzle on his lap, and he shook his head. "Neither of us belongs here, do we, dog?"

They sat together, staring at the fire. It crackled and put out heat, and Deacon let himself drift, trying to relax, to not care so damn much about every damn thing.

Damn. He'd been trying not to swear so much.

He petted the dog, letting her silky pelt ease his worries, and tried to figure out where he'd gone so wrong with Nora.

Probably agreeing to that first date.

The dog left him a few minutes later. Then Simon peeked his head in and waved.

"Hey, slacker." Deacon yawned. "Man, it's cozy in here." He shifted on the couch and tugged a throw over himself. "Think I'll take a little nap."

"I'm supposed to find you and remind you to take Oreo out." Simon grinned. "But since you've been covering for me today—"

"No shit."

Simon's grin widened. "Jenna and I will take out Oreo. And I won't tell anyone you're in here. I swear."

"Good. You owe me." He didn't know why he had to say it. "Your aunt was needling me again. She's so mean to me."

Simon nodded. "She is mean. I told you that a long time ago." The boy laughed. "She says I'm just like my mother, but Mom says I get my sarcasm from Nora." Simon studied him, looking for what, Deacon had no idea. "Anyway, you did me a solid. I'll do you one back. You can hide in here until dinner."

Before Deacon could say he hadn't been hiding, Simon closed the door, leaving him alone with flowers, books, the crackle of flames, and a very comfortable couch.

He sighed with pleasure and let himself relax. No work fires to put out, no family drama, no girlfriends to please. Just Deacon and the promise of a nap.

He closed his eyes and let himself go.

SIMON SHUT THE DOOR, TURNED AROUND, AND WATCHED HIS BEST friend play tug of war with Oreo's rope. Jenna and Simon had grown up together and been through a lot, including his inability to realize his crush on the girl had been returned. Now they called themselves boyfriend and girlfriend, though really not much had changed.

Well, if he didn't include the kissing parts. And those he liked a little too well to dismiss.

"What's that look for?" Jenna asked, crouched beside Simon's dog.

She wore jeans and a Riverdown High School sweatshirt, her dark brown hair pulled back in a ponytail. "Jealous I'm not playing tug-of-war with you?"

"Very funny."

"I would, but Oreo smells better." She laughed at him.

He laughed with her as they hunted down their jackets and boots and some doggie bags for Oreo's walk. Mitch's house—*no, my house,* Simon had to remind himself—sat on several acres of land away from neighbors and the main road with a killer view of the mountains. It took longer to get to school from the place, but the house had every-thing a guy could ask for.

Not only did Simon get to use the indoor pool, hot tub, and game room, he also had access to an amazing weight room, media room, and a big bedroom away from his mom and Mitch's. He loved seeing them hug, kiss, and hold hands—the normal kind of affection. But any hint of sexy action had to stay far away from him. Because that was just gross.

But even better than his parents loving each other and all the great stuff *inside* the house, outside it felt like he'd been dropped in the middle of the mountains, away from everyone. The house sat on a somewhat flat piece of land that gradually sloped up then down again, nestled between a few hills blocking them from the harsher winds from the mountains. The area behind the house had lawn for entertaining, like a football game or soccer. Mitch had even put in a practice quarterback training net, which he and Deacon liked to fool around with just for fun. Simon liked it, though he had no intention of becoming a QB, preferring the position of running back, like Mitch.

He held Jenna's hand as they followed Oreo bounding over the back lawn toward the woods bordering the yard. The property extended for what felt like a mile in all directions, all except for the driveway that led to the main road.

He loved it out here, where he could get away from everyone, enjoying his solitude.

"You're way too quiet." Jenna squeezed his hand. "You okay?" She tilted her head, and he had to kiss her.

He leaned down and pecked her on the lips, loving her blush.

"I can do that because I'm your boyfriend."

She mock-glared up at him, her lips quirking as she tried to hide her smile. "You can do that because I let you do that."

"Well, yeah."

"*And* because you're my boyfriend." She laughed. "You big idiot. I still can't believe you thought I liked someone else. Who else watches anime and romantic comedies *and* likes sports? You know the Hall-mark channel is one of your favorites. You can lie to your mom, but you can't lie to me."

"I know, I know. But keep it quiet about the romcoms, would you? The guys would never understand."

She chuckled. "Make it worth my while to keep quiet and I will." They walked together, following as Oreo had to sniff the same trees she sniffed every time they went out. She took forever, circling, sniffing, circling, then finally did her business.

"Man, she takes forever." Jenna cringed as Simon bagged up a mess and disposed of it in a receptacle bin Mitch had put out in the woods for that very reason. "You could just leave it out and let the rain and snow take care of it."

"Sometimes we run out here. See the trail? I don't want to track that back in the house."

"Ew, good point."

He continued to walk with her, following Oreo in the woods, not sure how to start.

Jenna tugged him to a standstill. "Okay, talk, buddy. I can tell the hamster fell off the wheel in your small brain."

He sighed. "We have a problem."

"We do?"

"It's Deacon." Simon used to call him coach and still did when on the field. But at home, Deacon was family. Calling him Uncle Deacon felt weird. Kind of like with Nora, since he normally ended up calling her by name unless trying to grab her attention. "He needs help."

Jenna's eyes brightened. "Our kind of help?"

"Yep. He and Nora are pathetic. They act like they don't like each other, but I see how they look at each other when they think no one is watching."

"Still?"

Simon nodded. "Yep. You'll see. Watch them at dinner and tell me what you think."

"Oh, I will." They started walking back toward the house. "Simon? This time let me think up something better than that stunt we almost pulled with my aunt and your mom and Mitch. The jealousy angle can backfire. With Deacon and all his girlfriends, I don't think making Nora jealous is going to work."

Simon nodded. "Good point. I know the guy is popular, but he's been crazy with all the dating lately."

"You mean the sex?"

Simon flushed. Sure, he was a guy and a teenager, but he didn't think he was ready for the heavy stuff yet.

"I love how red you get when I say the s-word," Jenna teased. "Relax. I don't want to talk about it—or *do it*," she emphasized, and he relaxed even more. "But your uncle seems to be a little girl crazy. Maybe he has a sex addiction or something."

Simon frowned. "I thought he was just lonely. You think it's about, um, physical needs or something?" He felt a little sick thinking about any of the adults he knew getting busy.

"Who knows? He could have a medical condition."

"There's a condition for that? For real?" She had to be messing with him.

"I saw it on TV. I guess it's real. Heck, you can be addicted to anything nowadays."

"Um. Okay. Sure."

"We need to cover all the bases before we put a plan in action. See what you can find out about Deacon. I'll study him and Nora at dinner and let you know what I think."

And no more talk about sex. "Good plan."

"Well, we didn't have to do much to get your mom and Mitch together, but Nora needs help. And she deserves to be happy. I love her."

"Me too. And I love Deacon. I think they'd be good together if they'd stop arguing or ignoring each other."

Jenna nodded. "Adults are so stupid sometimes. It's like they forget how to keep things simple."

"Tell me about it." They neared the house, and Simon saw his mom carrying his new sister. His heart felt full all over again, and he put an arm around Jenna's shoulders. "But some things they do pretty darn good. Want to hold my sister?"

Jenna smiled. "Boy, do I! And just think. If you're lucky, and we do this right, you can be an uncle next year to Nora's kid."

"One step at a time." Simon whistled for Oreo. "Now try not to be obvious about what we're up to."

"Me? You're the one who can't keep a secret."

"What? I am not." They entered, put their boots to the side, and hung up their jackets while Oreo barked at them to hurry up.

"Oh really? Who was it that told my youngest sister I had a boyfriend?"

"No way. That's not my fault. She overheard me talking to you on the phone."

"That's not what she said."

Simon shrugged. "She's nine and has a crush on me. She's lying."

"What?" Jenna's eyes bugged out.

"That's what Melinda told me." Jenna's middle sister. "Hey, I did nothing to make Joy like me. I'm just naturally loveable."

"Well, maybe to me." She shook her head. "No, Joy doesn't have a crush on you, and she doesn't snoop, not like Melly does." Jenna nodded. "Melly must like you, even though she calls you Simple Simon every time she talks about you."

"I'm Simply Superior. That's what I told her the last time I was over." Simon smiled. "Of course she likes me. She has good taste."

Jenna laughed. "Poor Melly. No wonder she looks constipated every time you're over. It's not that she hates you. She likes you."

Simon frowned. "Wait. Constipated?"

"Never mind. Focus, Simon. And not just on your stomach. We have a new mission."

He faced her and saluted. "Operation Quarterback Sneak—Christmas Style."

"That's a terrible name."

"I like it. We'll call it QSCS for short."

She rolled her eyes. "Boys make everything complicated."

Simon's mom overheard and turned to them, smiling. "Yes, Jenna, they do. But sometimes complicated can be good. Meet Ava, Simon's baby sister."

As Jenna carefully took Ava in her arms and cooed over the girl, Simon let his mom hug him tightly to her.

"I love you, Simon."

He let her hold on extra tight, because she needed it. "Aw, Mom. You don't have to be so mushy."

She laughed.

He hugged her back, because he needed it too.

CHAPTER 5

*N*ora went in search of Deacon and found him snoozing in the reading room. How cool was it that her cousin had a freaking *reading room* in her monstrosity of a house? When Deacon had asked if she'd ever want something this large to live in, she'd told him the truth. The house was too much for her, but she wouldn't mind something larger than her small, one-bedroom cottage. Though cute, it wouldn't be enough should she ever get married and have children.

Not like that would be happening any time soon.

Deacon let out a loud breath, and she tiptoed over to him. It was too bad he acted like such a clueless jerk because he really did look the part of her kind of Prince Charming. She liked her men big, and he had muscle to spare. A broad chest, big arms, and firm thighs. The blanket hid the lower half of him from view, but she had committed the image of that ass to memory.

She sighed.

He shifted, and she froze, not wanting to be caught ogling the man. In sleep, he looked approachable, softer. Awake, he seemed on guard, at least around her. His short hair framed a hard face, with a square jaw and firm lips. Yet his hair looked so soft…

She had to fight not to give in to temptation and touch it. Stupid. She'd put him out of her mind. Her lip service about forgiving him would make any chance meetings if not comfortable, at least not so excruciating. Nora had done the grownup thing for once and tried to be the better person.

She pasted a smile on her face. "Deacon, time for dinner."

He didn't move.

"Deacon," she said a little louder.

She frowned. His breathing seemed shallower, almost nonexistent. Was he okay?

She moved closer, repeating his name, but got no reaction. Alarmed, she leaned over him and put her hand on his forehead, thinking he felt warm.

Then he *moved* and yanked her down on top of him.

She opened her mouth to shriek, but nothing came out. Stunned by the speed of her capture, she lay over the man, wondering what to do next.

He opened his eyes and blinked up at her. "Nora?" His voice was hesitant, and he drew her closer, his hands holding hers pinned between them. "Am I awake?" he murmured.

"I, uh…" She couldn't look away from his face so close to hers. Then she did a very bad thing and let her gaze travel to those firm lips.

She couldn't say later who moved first, but her mouth pressed against his, and he was kissing her. *Boy,* was he kissing her.

It was so much better than she'd ever imagined. He took charge, capturing her mouth with his own. He released her hands to cup her cheeks and turned her head, deepening the angle of his kiss.

She was drowning in sensation, awash in shock and pleasure that she was kissing Deacon Flashman. Then the brute threaded his tongue between her lips and stole her ability to think.

One hand continued to hold her head in place while the other moved down her back and pressed her closer to him.

"Hmm. Nora," he whispered against her lips and kissed his way to her neck.

She tried to catch her breath, but Deacon grabbed her ass and ground up against her, and mother of mercy, but he was packing something large and insistent beneath that blanket.

He sucked on her neck, giving her a nip, and shocked her into jerking back.

She could see the moment he realized what he was doing. Nora wanted to rip him a new one, to adamantly deny any involvement in the kiss. But when his eyes narrowed, and he yanked her back to him for an angrier kiss, she met him nip for nip.

Devouring his mouth, grinding over him to get as close as humanly possible, she wanted to ride him until that tingling inside her erupted into a full-fledged *yes, yes, thank you God.*

Unfortunately, excited barking shocked her to stillness…and to a hard knock to the floor.

"Shit," he rasped. "Sorry, Nora. Are you okay?"

She blinked up at Deacon leaning over the couch to stare down at her in concern. Oreo bounded onto the cushions and started licking him all over.

"Stop it, Oreo. This dog…" He rolled back onto the couch then swore.

The dog leapt to the ground and started licking Nora everywhere she could reach. Nora couldn't help laughing, but Deacon's groan had her reassessing the situation.

"Are *you* okay?"

His face scrunched in pain, and his hands over his crotch hinted at what might have been the problem.

"That damn...dog...hit me...right... *God.*" He curled onto his side, turned toward the back cushions.

"Oreo!" Simon and Jenna stood at the doorway, staring inside.

Nora flushed, hoping they hadn't seen more than the dog mauling Deacon.

"Sorry," said Simon. "Wanted to let you guys know dinner's ready."

Nora harrumphed. "Your grandma told me I was supposed to get Deacon."

"Yeah, well, you're both late." Jenna hustled Simon away. "See you at the table. Come on, Oreo."

The teens and the dog left, and Nora had to wonder where the heck her brains had gone.

She slowly sat up and saw Deacon staring at her, still curled on the couch but now facing her. Fumbling for something to say, she said, "Uh, well, uh..."

"Yeah." He sat up with a wince.

"Oreo really nailed you, huh?"

"Yep." He shoved the blanket away and spread his thighs. "Jesus, she has a real kick."

Nora tried not to laugh.

"Go ahead, you know you want to."

She burst into laughter.

He didn't look amused, and that made her laugh even harder. "Sorry, sorry." She had to work to catch her breath.

"I'm sorry too." He pulled her up on the couch, sitting next to him. "I didn't mean to kiss you. Well, I did, but not at first."

Her face heated. "I was trying to wake you up for dinner."

"I'm awake now." He wiggled his brows.

"Shut up."

"I thought I was dreaming. I was sleeping, and then there you were, right on top of me."

She blushed even harder. "You surprised me when you yanked me down."

"Score."

"Deacon."

He grinned, and this open, playful side of him had her heart racing more than usual around him.

"I really didn't mean to assault you." He cleared his throat. "I'm sorry that—"

"You didn't assault me," she snapped, not liking the apology. "It was an accidental kiss." *And yes, that makes no sense, Nora.* "If anything, *I* assaulted *you.*"

His eyes narrowed. "That's true. You did."

"I— Wait. You're agreeing with me?"

"I was sleeping. That's my excuse."

"No way," she denied. "You kissed me that second time, buddy."

He ignored her. "At first, I was dreaming about you, and then there you were."

"You were dreaming about me?" *That's flattering. I wonder if his dreams are anything like mine.*

He nodded, and her heart skipped. "I dream about you a lot. Nightmares, usually. You're typically impaling me on something. A knife, an ax, a sword. I'll be on the verge of death while you strut around in black or red, usually something see-through and sexy, and—"

"Very funny."

He grinned. "So for me to see my sexy nightmare so close, I had to make the first move."

"By kissing me?" By now, her entire face had to be cherry-red.

"I don't know. I had to do something. The kiss felt good. Too good." He watched her. "I realized it wasn't a dream, and then you attacked me."

"Maybe you attacked me." She couldn't remember who had moved first, but that angry kiss was as hot if not hotter than the dream kiss.

"You just said you—"

"Never mind. Let's forget about it."

He grabbed her hand before she could leap off the couch. "Wait. Look, I'm sorry. I didn't mean to kiss you and dump you to the floor. And I was teasing about the nightmares."

Great. Now he was sorry they'd kissed.

He watched her with an odd look.

"What now?" She sighed.

"I hadn't realized your lips would be so soft."

They sat in silence, staring at each other.

Nora wanted to kiss him again. The ghosting, excuse-making, sexy-as-all-get-out football coach every available woman in town wanted to date.

No way.

She darted to her feet and hurried to the door. "This never happened. Now let's have a nice Thanksgiving. And we never mention this again."

NORA LEFT HIM SITTING ON THE COUCH, STARING AFTER HER LIKE AN idiot. He still didn't know what had just happened. His dream of playing house with his sexy sister-in-law—not technically, but she and Becca were as much sisters as he and Mitch were brothers—had become real.

When she'd pulled back, he'd realized the truth of the matter. And wanted her even more.

The passion she roused just by being mad was insane. And he did dream of her, too often. Imagining her touch paled next to the reality of Nora Nielson's incredible mouth. Firm, silky soft lips. A whisper of tongue stroking his. He'd been ready to move to the next step, sans clothes, in a heartbeat.

Especially because she gave as good as she got, teething his lips and practically devouring him on the couch. He wanted her right now, all over again, and wished he'd made his move those many months ago. Skipping out on her had been a huge mistake. And not just because she turned him on—*way* on—but because being around her made him like her all the more. Every time. Her kindness, her jeers, her sarcastic lens through which she viewed the world, all of it made him smile and feel good inside.

Good inside *all over* when they kissed.

"Oh man. Oreo, you are such a bad dog." He slowly stood, his body aching once more thanks to Nora's fine form, and took his time joining the others, taking care to think about anything but sexy Nora and her fine mouth.

Dinner passed with laughter and teasing. The teenagers watched him and Nora with a little too much interest, and he had a feeling they'd seen more of that kiss than he'd initially suspected. Time to stop that train of trouble before it got started.

Oreo managed to sneak a huge turkey leg from the kitchen, and they all laughed as Brenda tried unsuccessfully to run the dog down.

"Great training you're doing there with that pup," their father said to Mitch with a lot of sarcasm.

Nora snorted. "Right? Nice discipline. No wonder Simon gets away with everything."

Becca blinked. "I know you are not comparing the dog to my son."

"I sure am."

Jenna snickered, and Simon laughed.

Mitch's laughter turned to coughing when Becca arched a brow at him and said, "I know *you're* not laughing."

"No, dear." His fake submission encouraged more amusement. "I totally am," he murmured loudly enough for everyone else to hear.

Nora smirked, caught Deacon looking at her, and quickly looked away, her cheeks pink.

Out of the corner of his eye, Deacon caught Simon and Jenna nodding at each other.

Considering all the matchmaking attempts he, Nora, and Simon had made to get Mitch and Becca together, he figured he was due some teen meddling. But actually, the more he thought about the idea, the more it didn't bother him. Especially if it granted him the chance to change things with Nora, to let her see the real him and maybe get to know the real her.

"Hey, Bro, pass the potatoes for the fourth time." Mitch smacked him in the arm.

"Oh, sorry. Here." He glanced away from Nora and saw Becca looking at him with concern. "Sorry. I'm still a little fuzzy from my nap."

"Ha. Now you know what it's like to get old," his father barked. "Naps are a luxury."

"Amen to that," Nora's father said and winked at Deacon.

"I was dreaming about this demon trying to steal my soul. She was really pretty and really evil."

"Hmm. Sounds like someone we all know," Mitch teased, looking at Nora.

"Suck it, Flashman."

"Nora," her mother scolded.

Mitch and his dad laughed it up while Luke, her dad, tried not to encourage his daughter but couldn't keep from grinning.

"Oh yeah, Simon. That's where you get your mouth from," Mitch said.

Becca nodded. "Told you."

"Anyway," Deacon interrupted, enthralled with how beautiful Nora was as she blushed and laughed while trying to maintain that death glare she kept aiming his way. "The demon was right there, hovering over me, demanding my soul… Then I looked up and saw Nora, and damn if I didn't think I was still dreaming."

"Nice, Deacon." Nora scowled.

"I only meant because the demon in my dream was beautiful, and then I saw you and thought you had to be the same person because you're so pretty, Nora."

The entire table went silent. Everyone looked from Nora to Deacon and back.

"Quit teasing." Nora stabbed her turkey and pointed her knife his way. "You are such an ass."

Mitch chuckled. "Yeah, he's a Flashman all right. Charming, right Mom?"

Brenda sighed. "Sorry, Nora. I blame Lee for my sons' shortcomings."

Lee looked puzzled. "He called her beautiful. I think that's nice."

"Thanks, Dad."

Nora's mom, Sue, did her best to try to hide laughter. "Um, Lee, I think it's Deacon's comparison of Nora to a demon that's not so nice."

Lee frowned. "Well, I guess. But he did say she's beautiful, and she certainly is."

Nora stared at her plate, chewing with concentration.

Sue smiled. "That's so sweet, Lee."

Brenda guffawed. "Now who's blushing?"

"Hush, woman."

Deacon met Mitch's amused gaze and shrugged. Becca left the table and returned with Ava, and talk turned to babies and the coming Christmas holiday. But he caught Nora's eye and saw her drag a finger across her throat and point at him, which had him laughing so hard he nearly choked on his stuffing.

CHAPTER 6

*H*ours later, the family had feasted, cleaned up, and played their requisite board game. After being trounced by Nora and her allies several times, Deacon took a break and helped Mitch select a movie for them all to watch before turning in for the night.

Their dad and Simon had run Jenna home, and Nora entered the media room holding Ava. She looked so pretty, smiling with a baby in her arms, so natural.

So right.

She glanced up and caught him looking at her, but for once, she didn't growl, snarl, or dart him threatening looks. She continued to smile. Joyful, kind, and so damn beautiful his heart threatened to burst from his chest. He hastily looked back at Mitch and stumbled through an answer to whatever Mitch had asked him.

When he next glanced up, Nora had left, and Mitch was groaning.

"What's your problem?"

"I swear, you screw this up again, you are out of the family."

Deacon frowned. "What?"

"You and Nora. Quit messing around and ask her out on a date. A real date, not to swing through Mickey D's for a gourmet meal followed by a quickie at *chez* Flashman."

"You're not funny. At all."

"And you're not fooling anyone about how you feel about Nora. Make a move or get out of the race, son."

"I'm not your son, asswipe. And I have no idea what you're talking about."

"God save me from stupid people."

Becca entered with Ava in her arms. "I thought that was my line. And it's stupid *men*, not stupid people, honey."

Deacon sank into a plush recliner and sighed. "Becca, he's bullying me again. Let me hold the baby while you yell at him." He took Ava in his arms and marveled at her baby smell and tiny fingers and toes. He rested her against his chest and felt her squirm, and his heart seemed to expand inside him. His perfect niece was wonderful.

He cuddled her and felt warm all over. "Someday, Ava, you'll throw a football, and your entire world will be right. I'll teach you how to pass and run plays. You'll love it. It takes a lot more brains to organize plays than to catch a ball and run down a football field."

"Hey." Mitch glared.

"Then you'll learn how to craft a decent IPA, and you'll really be rocking."

Nora entered and grinned. "Stop polluting that poor girl with nonsense. Baby Ava will write books and become a bestseller when not making amazing new recipes for her cooking show, right Becca?"

"That's right." Becca snuggled up with Mitch in a seat.

Nora sat on the arm of Deacon's chair, her hand over the baby's small head, and Deacon felt weird, as if he was seeing a future that might one day be his, if only he had the courage to reach for an impossible dream.

He looked up and saw Nora staring down at him, a challenge in her chocolate-brown eyes.

"Got a problem with that, Flashman?"

"No," he murmured. "You know, I don't think I do."

"Huh?"

"And like that, our little bird is ready to fly and be on his own," Mitch said in a mock whisper.

Nora turned to him. "What's that?"

"Nothing." Becca punched her husband in the chest.

"Ow."

"Stop baiting your brother and Nora," Becca warned him. "Uncle Luke and Aunt Sue are hot tubbing it, and they said to go ahead and watch the movie without them."

Mitch protested, "We should wait."

Nora sat next to Deacon, taking the chair between him and Mitch. "Let them have a date night. I can't remember the last time my parents were near a hot tub in a romantic setting."

"Oh, are you angling for a little brother or sister for yourself, Nora?" Deacon teased, in no hurry to give Ava back. She really wasn't any bigger than a football.

Nora grimaced. "No. And I wish you'd stop putting weird images in my head."

He chuckled.

She continued, "Because your parents seem pretty lovey-dovey. I bet they'd be happy to make you and Mitch another—"

"Press play, Mitch," Deacon interrupted.

"You don't have to tell me twice." Mitch pressed a few buttons. The lights went down, and a movie appeared on the screen.

Deacon turned to Nora. "Little Bro once caught an eyeful of the parents on a 'date night.' Hasn't been the same since."

Mitch groaned.

Nora sighed. "Poor guy. Been there, done that. Got the trauma to prove it."

Simon walked in.

"And speaking of trauma…"

"Hey, are you guys watching a movie without me?"

"It's a romantic comedy," Becca warned.

Simon sighed. "I'll stay, but only because Grandpa Lee is going to bed and everyone else is in the hot tub."

"Everyone, huh?" Deacon muttered, hoping to get a rise out of Nora. "Hadn't realized Mom was into threesomes."

"What did you say?" Simon asked, but Nora had been taking a drink and choked on it.

"You okay?"

She drank to calm herself, then couldn't help shaking her head. "You're evil."

He smiled. "Takes one to know one."

"Ass."

Mitch sighed. "We really do need to change your name to the one most people use for you."

Simon grinned. "Uncle Ass. It has a nice ring to it."

"Simon Bragg, you watch your mouth."

"Yes, Mom."

Deacon and Nora exchanged a knowing look. "Ah, the power of the mom."

Becca grinned at her cousin. "You ought to try it, Nora. I have a feeling you'd be pretty darn good at it."

Nora glanced from the baby to Deacon and flushed. "Someday, maybe. Now let's all hush up and watch the movie." Before Deacon could say something funny, she put a hand over his mouth. "And not one more word out of you."

He winked, and when she took her hand away, nodded with mirth. "I hear, and I obey."

"If only."

FIVE DAYS AFTER THEIR THANKSGIVING FEAST, THE SNOW DECIDED TO fall and keep falling. Nora stood in Bragg's Tea, helping out during the winter hours while Becca bonded with her new addition to the family. When Nora could finally catch a break after a grueling three hours of nonstop traffic, she leaned down to set her elbows on the counter, her chin in her hands, and watched fat, white flakes of snow continue to fall.

"It's so pretty, isn't it?" Jenna sighed. The girl worked part-time now that the soccer season had ended. And if Nora was honest, she did a better job than Simon at interacting with customers. Jenna had a sweet though direct vibe Nora enjoyed, while Simon was naturally nice to everyone, taking his mother's "the customer is always right" to heart. Whatever. Nora tried to be pleasant, but she had no time for asshats.

"Nora?" Jenna said. "You okay?"

"Yeah, the snow is great." Nora glumly watched the customers enjoy their drinks and treats while Jenna stocked more loose leaf tea on the shelves. In the back, Ruth was baking scones and cookies, and the sweet smells mixed with the holiday music and falling snow outside. It should have felt like a winter wonderland. The slew of customers continued to prove that though it might be early in December, many had decided to load up on caffeine and sweets for the holiday season. They'd need to restock the specialty teapots and mugs at the front of the store as well.

She mentioned as much to Jenna, who took the task with pleasure. Jenna loved keeping busy.

Nora normally did as well, but she'd been feeling so strange since Thanksgiving with the family. So...lost.

That kiss with Deacon continued to replay in her mind, and she knew she'd made a huge mistake. Then she'd remember how lovely it had felt to hold Ava, how she'd watched Becca and Mitch, so in love, Simon thrilled with his family.

Nora didn't have that. And to be honest, she'd never have that if Deacon kept taking so much space in her thoughts. She needed a break. Something had to shift in her humdrum of a life.

Jenna returned to the counter just as the bell over the door jingled, signaling more customers. "Hey, Nora. What are you doing for your birthday this year?"

"I'm aging. That's what I'm doing." Turing thirty-five, no baby, no husband or boyfriend, no new prospects with her career. She'd become the personification of boring, somehow. Where had Nora's dreams gone? Of writing that great novel? Of finding love and starting her own family?

She loved being the fun aunt. But for God's sake, when would she finally have special people to call her own? Two years ago she'd been secretly engaged for all of a few weeks, until she and her intended had realized they'd wanted different things. They'd impulsively gotten engaged, tired of being the lone single person among friends and family.

She didn't miss Flynn at all, though he'd been a nice and funny guy. Now a nice, funny, and *married* guy traveling the world, or so his social media posts would have her believe.

Depressed and trying to hide it, she straightened, pretending she didn't see Jenna's concern. "Sorry for being a downer. I'm tired, and my feet hurt. But I do plan to splurge on Christmas Eve. I'm talking eggnog, sugar cookies, and Christmas movies until I puke."

"Um, er, that sounds like fun." Jenna would have said more, but a familiar voice had them both turning to the new customer.

"Whoa. Smells amazing in here." Deacon and some pretty blond stood side by side. "Hi Jenna. How's it going?"

Jenna answered him, making small talk with the couple.

Typical Deacon. Nora didn't know why she should feel hurt that he had a new lady in his life. Heck, new? For all Nora knew, Deacon had been dating the woman while canoodling with Nora during Thanksgiving.

She forced herself to act as if it didn't matter. Because it didn't. "Hi there." *Jackass.* "What can we get you?" She wanted to punch him for looking at her with warmth and a flare of attraction he apparently felt he didn't have to hide. What a jerk. Feeling sorry for his girlfriend, she gave the woman a smile. "We have gingerbread cookies a few minutes from coming out of the oven, and everything behind the glass is fresh as well. We've been selling like crazy today."

The woman grinned. "Oh wow. I have to have a gingerbread man. No, make it two. Three."

Deacon snorted. "Woman, you need a sugar intervention."

"As if you should talk. I saw all the food you put away at breakfast, and yeah, I saw the sweet roll you pretended you ordered for me. It's not fair that you have an abnormal metabolism."

They'd shared breakfast. *God.* And he'd brought the woman here? Why? To flaunt her in Nora's face? Or maybe to show Nora she shouldn't make anything out of their one and only time kissing? *Well, no problem, bucko.*

She gave him a subtle glare he couldn't miss.

But instead of taking him aback, he smiled wider. "We'll take *six* gingerbread men and two peppermint cocoas." He looked behind him then turned back around. "No, three peppermint cocoas. And add a warm milk, would you?"

"I'm grabbing a table," said a man from behind them.

Nora saw a good-looking man Deacon's age. He had medium brown skin and an engaging smile, his eyes as bright as the eyes of the little boy he held.

Deacon said over his shoulder, "The kid seats are in the corner." He turned his attention back to Nora and Jenna. "Ladies, meet Jess. Her husband and I co-own River Rip Brewery. Roy, Jess's ball and chain, is carrying the cute tyke, who happens to be my godson, Chris."

Jess held out a hand. "Hi, Nora. I've heard so much about you."

Nora shook her hand, her suspicion clear. "None of it good, I'm sure."

Jess laughed. "All good, I promise. Deacon was telling us how much you've been helping your cousin and Mitch since they just had a baby. I had Chris in Houston with my parents close-by. I don't know what we would have done without them." She leaned closer. "Roy's parents are not kid friendly."

"I heard that," Roy called from a table a few feet from the counter.

"Has ears like a bat," Deacon muttered. "Well, get us our food, woman."

"I *know* you're not talking to me." Nora scowled.

"I thought the customer was always right?"

Jenna snickered. "Only when Simon or Zoe are working the counter. Nora and I like to think *we're* always right. Obnoxious customers get the boot."

"I like this place." Jess grinned. "I've actually been in before, but it's been a while since I've had time to swing by. Great to meet you guys. And Deacon..." She punched him in the arm. "Behave. If I don't get my cookies, I'm not going to be pleasant to be around."

Deacon winced, especially when his buddy called out, "Be nice, idiot."

"I like your friends." Nora waited while Jenna fetched their drinks.

"You would," he said, still studying her. "You look good."

"Yes, I do."

He paused, as if not sure how to respond. "So, ah, how have you been?"

"Alive and breathing. You?"

He shrugged. "Busy. We've been getting a ton of customers since we did some new advertising, and we're starting to get really busy at night now. Roy brought in some great bands." He watched her. "You should swing by some night. I'll even give you a beer on the house."

"For my date too?" She had no idea why she threw that out there, but seeing him stiffen made her feel better.

"Date?"

"Yes, date—a four letter word for a romantic partner."

Jenna returned with his cocoas on a tray. "Or a fruit."

Nora turned to her. "A date isn't a fruit. Is it?"

Jenna nodded. "It's the fruit of a date palm tree. I just did a report on it in biology."

Deacon took the drinks and delivered them to his friends before returning. "Jenna, go away."

She left with a salute.

Nora made a mental note to have a stern talking-to with the teen for obeying the enemy. "Your cookies are coming right up." She darted into the back and returned with a tray of just-out-of-the-oven cookies she slid into the glass case. After retrieving his on a plate, she warmed up a glass of milk and set it all on a tray. "They smell terrific."

He just looked at her. "You know what? I'm good with that."

"Huh?"

"Bring your date if you want. The more the merrier."

She frowned, feeling as if he'd called her bluff, though she hadn't expressly said she'd be bringing anyone. "I didn't say I had a date. It was a hypothetical question. Oh, sorry. That's a big word for you." She heard Jenna laugh behind her. "A what-if kind of question."

He smirked, which increased her irritation. "Look, we're always happy to have more customers at the pub. You could bring a date, a friend, or family." He paused. "Or come by yourself. I'm sure I can keep you company."

She frowned. "Are you coming on to me?"

He laughed. "Don't hold back, Nora."

He frustrated the crap out of her by saying nothing more, just watching her. And his handsome factor kept doubling. He wore arrogance like some men wore designer clothes. It made him look both fascinatingly attractive and untouchable. A bad boy now holding a tray of cookies and warm milk.

She cleared her throat. "That'll be fifteen bucks, buddy."

"You're so pretty, Nora."

She blushed. "Pretty annoyed with your attitude." She crossed her arms over her chest. "I'd better get a big tip."

He paid, giving her an extra three dollars for doing no more than fetching his order. "Oh, and that's for Jenna. For you I leave my smile." He showed a lot of pearly whites.

"I'll tell you where you can put that smile," she muttered.

"Deacon, come on. Roy is getting crabby," Jess announced.

"I thought Chris was the baby," Nora said.

"He is." Deacon sighed. "But Roy's a huge pain when his blood sugar gets low."

"Oh, so it that your excuse too?"

"You always have a snappy comeback. It's one of the things I like best about you."

He left on that note, and she stared after him, confused, in lust, and feeling as if up had become down. Which maddened her to no end, because she thought she'd convinced herself to be done mooning over the man.

Instead, she watched him chat up his best friend, his best friend's wife, and fawn over the cutest little boy.

Nope. She definitely needed to get her head on straight. And maybe figure out where her boring life was leading her. Like maybe somewhere far away from this town and the handsome idiots in it.

CHAPTER 7

"What the heck did you say to piss her off?" Roy sipped from his mug of cocoa. "Oh man, this is good."

Jess nodded. "They make the best hot chocolate."

"You should try their sticky buns." Deacon moaned. "So good. Too bad Becca is out with the baby or you'd be eating a few right now."

Roy looked past him to the counter, where Nora chatted up the next customer. "She looks so much happier talking to that woman than she did talking to you."

Jess grinned behind her mug.

"I see that." Deacon frowned. "I don't know. I can't seem to say anything right around Nora. I called her pretty. She said she was pretty annoyed with my attitude."

Jess flat out laughed. Roy smirked.

"Oh, shut up you two."

"For once, you're not the one being pursued. Is that why you like her so much?" Jess asked.

He shushed her, conscious of teenage Jenna hanging close by their table, eavesdropping and making no attempt to hide it. He shot an accusing stare Roy's way. He'd confided to Roy his weird feelings for Nora, that maybe he liked her because she didn't seem to like him back.

"Sorry, man." Roy shrugged. "I have to tell Jess everything. If I don't, she somehow knows. Then I'm sleeping on the couch."

"You got that right." Jess clicked her mug against Roy's. "Deacon, she seems to like you. I can tell. Even if she did seem a little irritated."

He glared at Roy. "See if I tell you anything ever again."

Roy at least had the sense to look shamefaced. "I can't help it. I'm weak. I admit it."

"Yes, I own him, body and soul." Jess looked wicked as she eyeballed her husband. "And you, dear, are getting *so* lucky later tonight."

"Jess, the children!" Deacon put his hands over Chris's ears, causing Chris to belly-laugh. He tickled the boy, so in love with yet another tiny person. His godson. Man, since when was he so into babies? He shot a subtle glance Nora's way, pleased to see her watching him.

When she saw him looking back, she frowned.

He smiled and waved.

Her expression grew darker.

Why that made him happy, he had no idea. "I don't know how to get her to talk to me."

"She was just talking to you, man."

Jess and Deacon shared a look, and Jess explained to her clueless husband, "Remember when we first started dating? And I didn't want to give you the time of day?"

"Yeah, you were so into me but trying to hide it. Girls are weird."

"Hey, genius, you were dating two girls at the same time."

"They knew about each other. I'm no—" he glanced at his son and nodded to Deacon, who covered Chris's ears again "—man whore."

"Please." Jess snorted, and Roy laughed at her. "You totally were. The best looking guy in high school who got any girl he wanted."

"Is that why you played hard to get?"

"I had to wait until your ego popped and you fell back to earth. You're lucky I agreed to go out with you."

"I know."

Deacon loved watching his friends play-argue. He could feel the love between them, and it was real. "Yeah, Roy, we all know. You won the lottery with this one. Of course, that was after she and I dated first."

Roy stopped chewing and gaped at them. "What?"

"Don't choke." Deacon smirked. "I'm kidding. We were friends. She was tutoring me in chemistry, and I threw you a bone, talking you up, telling her how you'd matured since high school. You're welcome."

"Oh please. I was the one doing the hunting." Jess looked smug. "The truth is, *I* snared *you*, Roy Thompson. Like a helpless rabbit."

"You do look a little wolf-like," Roy noted, now smiling.

Chris started fretting, so Deacon lifted him into his arms without being asked. He'd been helping and dealing with the kid ever since Roy and Jess had come back from Houston with their son. He felt like a super uncle, dealing with a teenage Simon, a toddler, and now Baby Ava.

"My point, Deacon," Jess said, "is that you're just like Roy. A man-you-know-what." She held her arms out for Chris, and Deacon handed off the boy. "But unfortunately, you have no one backing you up. Mitch is useless. He's your brother."

"He is useless," Deacon agreed.

"I just mean he's your brother, so he's obviously biased. If he tells Nora how great you are, she won't believe him."

"I'm trying to do this on my own." He glared at the happy couple. "I told Roy about my problems—*in confidence*—and after running to you and blabbing, you now apparently think you can help me out with the ladies. I mean, it's me. Deacon Flashman. Do you think I need help?"

The teenage eavesdropper passed by and said, "Yes, you need as much help as you can get."

Roy toasted her before turning back to Deacon. "Your lady is not giving you loving looks. In fact, if looks could kill..."

Deacon sighed. "I'm really into mean-Nora. She's so hot."

"Ew. Is this going to be a guy sex talk or something?" Jess cringed.

"I've been having such realistic dreams, lately," Deacon said just to tease Jess. "You know the kind I'm talking about, Roy."

"Oh, man."

"Please, no more." Jess stood with Chris. "I'm taking my innocent baby to the restroom."

Deacon nodded. "Good, because he stinks."

Roy laughed at his wife's huff. "He does, babe. Sorry. But it's your turn."

"Men." Jess left to change the boy.

Roy turned to Deacon. "You want my advice? Wear your girl down." He nodded to Nora at the counter with new customers. "It worked with Jess. Despite all that nonsense you spouted about me being a good guy, I had a plan that nabbed me the girl."

"Huh. Not the way Jess tells it."

"She has no idea about my finer skills with subtlety."

"Apparently, I don't either," Deacon said wryly.

"Funny. Look, man, this will work. With Jess, I was just always there. I think she went out with me to get me to go away." He grinned, and Deacon chuckled. "I'm serious. Try that with Nora. You said she's everything you think you want in a woman, right? You already know she's no Rhonda."

Deacon hated that he inwardly cringed at his ex's name. "I wish I didn't still think of Rhonda. It's like she's a poison slowly working her way out of my system. I mean, it's been three years already."

Roy grimaced. "Yeah, but she was larger than life and nasty. You're good now."

Deacon held up his mug. "Thanks to you."

Roy brightened. "Yeah, I healed you. Hell, I saved you. You have to name your first kid Roy."

Deacon chuckled, and his gaze automatically sought Nora. "How about I slip Roy in as a middle name?"

When Roy didn't respond, Deacon glanced back to see his friend staring at him. "What?"

"You're thinking about having kids?" Roy looked from Deacon to Nora and back again, shocked.

Deacon flushed. "Not yet. I mean, I need the right woman first. It's just with all the babies around, it's impossible not to think about them."

"Sure. Right." Roy looked back at Nora. "Just remember what I said. The whole wear 'em down strategy is gold. And it's not stalking if you just happen to be shopping or walking around near them. Don't engage. Just be there. Let her see you without talking to her. Or looking at her."

"Um, is this advice a lawyer once gave you?"

"Maybe." At the look Deacon shot him, Roy rolled his eyes. "No,

Gigantor. I'm kidding. I'd say be yourself, but that doesn't seem to be working. Try it my way." His gaze went to Jess and Chris, emerging from the hallway. "It worked for me."

"Yeah, you lucky bastard. It did."

"And the middle name sticks. Girl or boy. Swear it."

Deacon gave him a swear all right. But what Roy had said stuck. He'd give it a go and see…

NORA GLARED AT THE LARGE SHADOW SHE SEEMED TO HAVE ACQUIRED.

Ever since seeing Deacon in the tea shop five days ago, she seemed to be running into him all over town. As her week had progressed, work and shopping bogged her down. She spent all her time either between the tea shop and home, writing, or out getting gifts. She'd grown tired.

The Christmas season didn't have the same appeal it had had last year. Or the year before that. Heck, for the last few years she'd been less than festive.

It felt as if each passing year, in which Nora remained stagnant and alone, grew harder to bear.

Seeing Becca's happiness only made it worse. Becca not only worked at her dream job, she had a dream of a family. Nora's envy was like a spike deep inside, causing emotional pain. And that bitterness grew. She knew it was unhealthy but couldn't help her feelings, because Nora was no closer to finding a man or getting her dream job going— writing that book she'd been working on for years.

Recently, she'd started looking at housing prices in Salem, Portland, and even Seattle. Perhaps moving away from the past would help her start a fresh future and kick her into doing something with her life?

She didn't know, but something had to give, and soon. Nora felt as if on an emotional roller coaster, happy one day, crabby or sad the next. And she knew it had nothing to do with that time of the month and everything to do with a certain unavailable someone she kept running into at the oddest times.

As she walked around Hope's Pond downtown, trying to enjoy the snow frosted trees and holiday lights in the snowy evening, she passed couples and families, not helping her mood any.

Then to see the man partly responsible for her relationship quandary suddenly in front of her... She'd seen him often over the past few days. Always close by but not close enough to confront. She'd waved once, and he'd seemed startled to see her, so she'd felt like an idiot.

Or did he somehow think she was following him? How embarrassing. She felt her cheeks heat and ducked, hoping he'd keep looking at the pond and the starry sky and ignore her passing by.

"Nora?"

Shoot. She glanced up and pretended a look of surprise. "Oh, ah, hi, Deacon. What are you doing out here?"

He glanced around and gave a satisfied groan that had her body taking notice. "Just appreciating the season. I don't get out as much as I should. Roy told me to stop being a bitch and take the night off, so I did."

She grinned. "I liked Roy and his family. What a cute kid."

Deacon smiled, the dimple in his cheek her undoing. She quickly looked at the sparkling ice of the pond, reflecting the moon and stars overhead.

"I like to tell Roy his son takes after me. Nurture over nature, right?" He turned and fell into step beside her. "You mind if I walk with you?"

"Um, sure. Fine."

"I met Roy and Jess in college," he said as they followed the trail around the pond. "Roy and I played college ball together. He could have gone pro, but he wanted Jess and a family instead. Took them a while, but now my little man, Chris, is their whole world."

"You and Roy have been friends for a long time then."

"Yep. He was there through a lot of my problems. A real great guy."

She wanted badly to ask but didn't feel it her place, so she kept her questions about his hard times and his failed marriage to herself.

"So, ah, are you dating anyone?" Deacon asked, out of the blue. "I mean, if you were, you might want to come by the pub this weekend. We have an incredible band playing Saturday night."

"Oh, thanks." She kicked the snow as they walked, feeling both unsettled yet protected by his large presence. He kept close to her when others passed, making them go around instead of bumping into her. Many smiled or nodded to him, and she realized what a popular man Deacon must be. "You seem to know a lot of people."

He sighed. "I try to keep a low profile. But everyone knows Mitch, and they know I'm his brother."

"Isn't that the other way around? They knew you before Mitch."

"Maybe at first, but he's done a lot to help this town since moving in. And marrying Becca, who also seems to know everyone, has only made him more popular."

Nora couldn't be sure, but she thought she detected an odd tone to his words. "Does that bother you?" she blurted before she could rethink her curiosity.

He blinked down at her. "Ah, well, a little." He shoved his hands in his jacket pockets and glanced away from her. "It's not easy being the big brother who failed. Compared to Mitch, I'm a two-time loser."

"What?" She stopped him in his tracks. "You're kidding right?"

He flushed. "I'm kidding."

She gaped. "Oh my God. You really feel that way."

He tried to walk away. "Forget I said anything. I'm tired. It's been a long day."

"No, wait." She tugged him to a stop again. "I get you. Really."

He looked down at her, his eyes dark, searching.

"I sometimes feel that way about Becca."

"What?"

Nora nodded, not sure why so much honesty seemed to be pouring out of her. "It's tough. We grew up like sisters, close, but even closer once she met and married Neal. She had a wonderful husband and an awesome son. Then Neal died, and the guys lined up for her. I mean, she's beautiful and sweet, and she had this cloud of sorrow around her."

Deacon nodded.

"I felt so bad for her. Then I felt jealous, because she had a perfect love and this perfect, tragic backstory." She blushed. "I sound horrible.'

"You do." He nodded. "I feel the same way."

"Horrified?"

"Yep, because I used to wish I was as successful as my little brother. It's hell on a guy's ego."

"Oh, yeah." So odd that they'd have jealousy over family in common. "Then Becca met Mitch, and she got another shot at a perfect family and life. And I'm so incredibly happy for her. No one deserves it more than her."

"But you wish you had that too." He sighed. "I understand." They started walking again, and he confessed, "My ex-wife was awful. Suffice it to say she hurt me when I was down, making it all worse. The divorce seemed to go on forever, several years, actually. And while I was trying to get a leg up, my little brother was winning Super Bowls, dating whoever he wanted, and making a fortune. I didn't care about the money so much. But man, I missed the game."

"I'll bet." She listened, learning so much about Deacon she never would have guessed.

"Anyway, not to make this a big pity party. I'm just saying I know how you feel. I'm really glad Mitch found Becca and that's he's so happy."

They walked in silence for a stretch, and Nora could feel his gaze on her. She glanced up, met his stare, and quickly looked away, blushing for no reason.

"So you're not dating anyone right now, is that what you said?"

It took her brain a moment to process his question. "Um, no. I'm not." She cleared her throat. "What about you? Got friends to take to the pub?"

"Nah."

She studied him, curious. "I thought you were with a girlfriend for Thanksgiving?"

"Didn't work out."

"None of your girlfriends seem to work out."

"Oh? Been keeping tabs, have we?" His smile seemed more sharklike than friendly.

"I wasn't trying to. I overheard Mitch talking to Becca at our late-Thanksgiving. He thinks you keep picking the wrong type of woman." Lest he think she might be about to offer herself as a new option, she admitted, "I've done that. Been picking all the wrong guys. Not that there have been that many, but my options are limited."

"Why?"

"Huh?"

"Why limited? You're beautiful, smart, and together. You could have any guy you wanted."

She didn't know what to say to that, so she didn't respond.

"Seriously. I'm not blowing smoke up your ass. I mean it."

She laughed. "Thanks, Deacon." She saw another couple walk by, arm in arm, and glanced down at Deacon's large hand.

What the hell is wrong with me? This is Deacon, for goodness' sake!

She stuffed her hands in her pockets.

"Well?" he said

"Well what?"

He let out a breath. "This is the part where you say, Deacon, *you're* handsome, smart, and together too. You can have any woman *you* want."

"Seriously?"

He nodded. "Then you add, 'So if you really need a woman to make you feel like you matter, I guess I'll agree to a date with you.'"

She stopped in her tracks, and it seemed to take him a moment to realize she'd stopped. He turned to face her. "Is that a yes?"

Nora wanted to smack herself in the head for even considering they might have things in common. "That's a big fat no. We went out once. Then you ghosted me."

He frowned. "I thought we'd agreed to put that in the past."

"We did. But I'm not forgetting it. I learn from my mistakes." She stepped forward to poke him in his rock-hard chest. "And you, buddy, would have been a *huge* mistake." She walked past him, determined to stop wondering about the big lug.

"But isn't 'huge' a good thing? Bigger is better, right?" he asked as he caught up. "I'm kidding, Nora." He jerked her to a stop. "Please. I mean it. I'm just teasing. I know I was wrong."

"For?"

He sighed. "For not following up with a second date."

"Well, why didn't you?" she asked, frustrated that not knowing why he hadn't called still bothered her.

"I don't know."

But she felt that deep inside, he did. "When you figure it out, let me know. I'm going to finish my walk in peace. Alone." She left him behind, and this time he didn't follow her.

By the time she arrived home, she'd made up her mind.

Nora needed to make some major life changes. And she'd start with a change of scenery.

Tomorrow.

CHAPTER 8

*D*eacon knew he'd blown it with Nora again. He'd been doing so well and then... Bam. He'd moved too fast too soon.

Fuck.

He walked into the tea shop Tuesday afternoon, hoping to make amends.

"Hi, Ruth." That he knew all the employees on account of frequenting Becca's place so much didn't bother him. Becca really did make the best sticky buns.

"Hi, Deacon." The older woman smiled. "What can I get ya?"

"Is Nora in?"

She winked. "Ah, in for that kind of sweet, eh?"

"Sweet? Nora?"

Ruth guffawed. "Good one. Well, our Mistress of Sweetness is not in, I'm sorry to say. She's taking a week off."

"She is? I just saw her yesterday."

"I don't know what to tell you. I heard she's going out of town on some kind of work trip, I think. I don't know much about her writing business. Zoe and Mira are filling in."

"Thanks." That was worrisome. "Can I get a chai latte to go?"

"Sure thing, handsome."

After he paid for his drink and left, he sipped as he walked, wondering how to handle this new development. He hadn't planned on involving Mitch in his private affairs. Having talked to Roy had been bad enough, but Roy knew all about making mistakes. He and Jess hadn't always been so rosy and happily in love. They'd gone through their own rough patches.

Then too, Roy had seen Deacon at his lowest. Back when he'd been going through his divorce with Rhonda, dealing with an injury that would never truly heal, and wondering where his life headed, Deacon had thought about ending his pain permanently. Roy had talked him off the ledge. Roy had been there for him, back when Deacon had been too ashamed to confide in his family.

He still couldn't believe he'd told Nora about his jealousy issue, about feeling inferior to his younger brother.

Even more astounding, she'd admitted to him about similar feelings she had for Becca. He never would have guessed, not from the way she always seemed so happy and loving around her cousin. But he understood better than anyone how love could twist one up inside. How guilt and remorse and affection could grow dark inside a guy.

Damn. Even more evidence that he and Nora had something together.

It had been all he could do not to grab her hand during their walk around the lake. He'd seen her longing as she watched couples passing, could feel her loneliness—a mirror of his own.

He'd felt so close to her. As if they'd reached a mutual understanding.

And then he'd messed it all up by asking her out.

What to do?

He returned to work and took care of paperwork Roy and he kept handing off to each other. After finalizing some orders and paying suppliers, he left for the day. It was almost six, so he decided to go home.

And found Simon on his doorstep, looking worried.

SIMON WATCHED DEACON APPROACH AND DID HIS BEST TO STICK TO the script. Jenna had handled Nora yesterday, replacing her suitcase with one filled with clothes Jenna had personally chosen for Nora's isolated cabin vacation.

Personally, Simon understood his aunt wanting to get away. Sometimes family could be too much, and Nora had been raised an only child. Though she and his mom were as close as sisters, they had developed that bond in their late teens, and Nora still lived alone by choice, according to her.

Jenna thought him clueless and said Nora would have happily lived with a boyfriend or a husband and kids. That she wanted what his mom had. How the heck Jenna would know his aunt better than he did, he had no idea. But she was a girl. Aunt Nora was a girl. He'd let his smart girlfriend handle Nora.

Now Simon had to maneuver Deacon just where he wanted him. Deacon, unlike Mitch, seemed pretty sharp. Deacon had been the one to make things happen when Mitch and Simon's mom had been too slow to see that they loved each other.

So how was it Deacon couldn't see how well he fit Nora?

Simon shook his head. Adults were so stupid sometimes.

"Yo, Simon. What's up?" Deacon smiled and tussled his hair. As if

Simon were five. Then again, Deacon still had to look down to see Simon eye to eye. The guy was huge, with large muscles and a subtle toughness missing in his younger brother.

If Simon had to go up against one of the Flashman brothers, he'd rather fight Mitch. Deacon seemed like he'd fight dirty and not quit until his opponent was broken. Or dead.

"Hey, Deacon. Can I talk to you?'

Deacon frowned. "You okay? Sure, you can talk to me." He unlocked the door, and the pair went inside.

Simon loved Deacon's house. It was a lot smaller than the one Simon now lived in, but just as nice. The guy had a functional first floor, with bedrooms, a study, and a living and dining area. The kitchen looked as showy as the one in Mitch's—*my house now*, he reminded himself again—but smaller. But the downstairs was the real living space. The guy had an "entertaining basement" according to Simon's mom. Complete with a pool table, spare bedroom, and a large space he used as a weight room. The massive flatscreen TV was perfect for watching Sunday games, and the fireplace gave it a cozy feel.

French doors led to a decently-sized yard complete with a fire pit. It was the kind of place Simon had always wanted for himself and his mom, a place where he could hang out with friends in town and live it up in style. And then his mom had married a millionaire.

He grinned to himself and accepted the iced tea Deacon offered.

"Talk, kid." Deacon leaned against the kitchen island, his sweater rolled up to his elbows, revealing muscular forearms.

Simon looked down at his own and flexed, feeling like a beanpole. When he glanced up at Deacon, he saw the large man trying to hold back a grin.

Simon sighed. "Go ahead. Tell me I'll get bigger if I eat all my veggies and do all my homework. I just need to grow into my body, right?"

"That the speech your mom and Mitch keep giving you?"

"Yeah."

"Sorry, but it's true. I was like you in high school. Didn't start hitting my stride until college. But then, you've seen Mitch. He's still small and trying to get bigger. So sad."

Simon snickered.

"Okay, sport. What's the deal? Why do you look so stressed?"

"It's Aunt Nora." He watched for any telltale responses and wanted to crow with glee when Deacon showed immediate worry.

"Is she okay?"

"I don't think so." Simon paused, seeing Deacon's true feelings. The guy liked Simon's aunt. A lot. And Simon had decided to help bring Deacon into the family. The man needed someone like Nora to soften him, give him the feels the way Jenna gave Simon the feels. That good kind of gooey care that said a girl liked you. And since even Mitch agreed that his brother was clueless about finding a good woman, Simon planned to help the guy out.

"Well?" Deacon demanded. "And what do you know about this trip she took out of town?"

"That's the thing. I overheard her talking to Mom." A lie, but he'd roll with it. He had listened to Jenna describe her conversation with Nora before Nora had left town. "Nora's lonely, and she's trying to figure out what to do with her life. She's sad because she—" *wants a baby* might freak Deacon out.

"She what?"

"She wants some space from all of us, and she wants a boyfriend. Like, a life of her own. Not that she doesn't love us, but..."

Deacon sighed. "Yeah, I get it."

Jenna had been spot-on, as usual. Deacon seemed to feel the same way. "So I know where she went. To her parents' cabin up in the mountains. We're worried because it's been snowing a lot up there, and she doesn't have good tires."

"What?"

Jenna had been sure the tire excuse would appeal to a manly need to fix things. And Deacon, she'd said, was pretty manly.

"Yeah, her tires aren't the best. What if she gets stuck up there? The Wi-Fi is spotty. I know because we went up there two summers ago and I couldn't chat up any of my friends. It sucked."

"Huh." Deacon looked pensive, staring at Simon but not seeing him. "She went alone?"

Simon nodded. "My mom said she took a suitcase and some food. And I think a laptop. She said she was going up there to work. But what if she gets hurt or stuck? What if she has no reception to get help? You should go check on her."

Deacon focused on Simon. "*I* should, huh?"

"Yep."

"She might not like me interfering. I should probably call her folks and let them know."

"*No.*" Simon shook his head. "I mean, she wants space. Aunt Sue and Uncle Luke would just be bothering her."

Deacon chuckled. "But I wouldn't? She normally wants my head on a spike. Give it up, kid. You're trying to set me up with your aunt. I can tell."

"What?" Simon gave a weak laugh. "No. That's not... I mean, I would never... You..."

"Stop. You're pathetic. Besides, I'm already sold. Give me her direc-

80

tions, and I'll go up and check on her. *Just* check on her. I don't want her to hate me for barging in on her."

Simon relaxed. "She won't. We think she likes you."

"We?"

Simon quickly answered, "Mom and me."

"Uh-huh."

Simon coughed. "Um, can I use your bathroom?"

"You know where it is." Deacon ran a hand through his hair. "Damn. She will *not* be pleased to see me."

"She won't know how you knew to find her though."

"So?"

"Blame Mitch for sending you to check up on her. He owes you one for hooking him up with my mom."

"That's true."

"I'll be right back." Simon headed down the hallway and detoured into Deacon's room. He knew where things were, having snooped a few times during his stayovers. He found a duffel bag under Deacon's bed and started throwing clothes in. Lots of warm stuff, underwear and socks. Then he pulled open the nightstand and saw what he'd expected... a box of condoms.

Not thinking about it, he dumped the whole box in the bag and zipped it up. Then he hurried down the hall to the downstairs, raced down and outside, and chucked the bag in the back of Deacon's SUV. Having done that, he hustled back inside and up the stairs into the bathroom. To continue the charade, he flushed the toilet, washed his hands, and exited while trying to relax his breathing.

"Man, I though you fell in," Deacon teased.

Simon blushed and weakly said, "I had to go."

Deacon laughed. "Okay, Cyrano. I'll go make sure your aunt is okay and try my hand at making her hate me a little less. You and Jenna stay out of my business though. You get me?"

"What? Jenna?" At Deacon's look, he sighed. "Yeah, sure."

"You got a ride home?"

"Um, no. But you could drop me off on your way up to the cabin."

Deacon frowned. "I don't like driving in the dark up the mountain." His frown cleared. "But with it dark and snowy, your aunt wouldn't make me drive back right away." He nodded. "Not bad. Okay, kid, get in the vehicle. I just need to hit the grocery store on the way."

"Aw man. I hate shopping."

"Suck it up, princess. These groceries might save your poor aunt if she's all alone without eggs."

"Huh?'

"Just get in the SUV."

"Oh, uh, sure." Simon got in and prayed Deacon didn't look too hard at the bag he'd tucked away in the back. But hey, it was all for love. His aunt couldn't be too mad at him when she eventually learned he'd meddled, right? Because Aunt Nora always found out the truth about everything. Hmm. Maybe he should warn Deacon of that fact.

"And no whining if I don't buy you an energy drink. That crap will kill you."

Or not. Deacon could learn about Nora on his own. And God bless the poor guy who thought he could tell Nora not to have an energy drink. Heck, Deacon would be lucky to survive the verbal lashing. And if the insane guy thought to deny Nora her morning coffee, he clearly had a death wish.

NORA STARED IN CONFUSION AT THE CLOTHES THAT DIDN'T BELONG IN her suitcase. She'd packed flannels and comfy PJs for a week-long stay in the cabin. Not skin-tight jeans, clingy sweaters, lingerie, and her emergency thongs—the underwear she wore when going on a hope-to-get-lucky date. She hadn't had one of those in months.

She frowned, wondering how the heck she'd gotten these clothes instead of the ones she'd packed.

Jenna.

The teenager had been hanging around Nora at her house, ostensibly swinging by to get some last minute suggestions on helping with the receipts from work. Jenna had lingered until Nora had finally asked if she needed a ride home, to which Jenna had blushed and left soon after. The conniver must have used the old bathroom excuse to raid Nora's closet and replace her packed wardrobe with this, something Simon had once done as a lark.

Baffled, Nora had no idea what Jenna thought she might be doing. Nora planned to be alone at the cabin. The nearest neighbor was a good quarter mile away, the lights of that cabin viewed across the large lake between them.

The snow continued to fall, the temperature cold but only a few degrees below freezing. Not so bad considering the average lows at this time of year. She felt Christmassy, even without a tree. Nora had already unpacked her groceries and thought about making herself a cup of hot chocolate with whipped cream on top.

She had enough food to stay through Christmas had she wanted, a mess of unhealthy carbs and sweets along with some decent sustenance to accompany loads of self-pity, a few romance novels, and the Hallmark movies previously downloaded onto her laptop. So long as the electricity and hot water heater held up, she'd be perfectly set in her quest for time to reconsider her future.

Letting her loneliness out felt good, and she indulged in feeling sorry for herself. She thought about her many failures with relationships, her job, about being just shy of turning thirty-five, and sobbed for a few minutes while her emotions held center stage. Once she'd gotten that jag out of her system, she felt much better.

She went about preparing a meal of grilled cheese and tomato soup along with a glass of eggnog—because she could. As she prepared to dig in while watching *It's a Wonderful Life*, she saw lights outside. Headlights that didn't belong.

Her heart raced. Who the heck would be up here at this hour and along this isolated area? Thoughts of serial killers raced through her mind, and she quickly turned off all the lights, grabbed a butcher's knife from the kitchen, and huddled behind the door.

A loud knock startled her into a breathy shriek.

"Nora?"

She knew that muffled voice. Had he haunted her all the way up the mountain? "Deacon?"

"Nora, open up. It's cold out here."

She couldn't believe he'd followed her. No. No way.

"Nora!"

She opened the door, letting the heat out and a blast of snowflakes inside, and stared. "What the hell are you doing here?"

He pushed past her and shivered, rubbing his sweater-clad arms. "Nice to see you too." He took a good look around and nodded. "Love the fire. Oh, I see you have a plenty of wood. Great."

She quickly shut the door behind him and flipped on some lights. "Hold on. What the heck are you doing here?"

"People are worried about you."

"That doesn't explain what *you're* doing here. You're not people."

He frowned. "Yes, I am." He paused. "Is that a knife?"

She flushed and hurried to put the knife back. "Last night I made the mistake of watching a Christmas movie with a killer Santa then followed it with one about Krampus."

"Huh?"

"You know, Krampus, the anti-Santa. It was very dark, and he had horns… Never mind." She hated that she'd succumbed to babbling. But geez, he sure did fill out that dark green sweater nicely. His chest looked so broad, his arms so thick.

"Weird, but okay." His gaze followed her from her head to her toes, pausing at her breasts before settling on her face. "You look good. Damn good."

She hated that her body reacted. "Deacon. Flashman. If you make me say 'my eyes are up here'" —she pointed to her eyes— "I will stab you with that knife."

"Whoa." He held his hands up. "I give up. Have your way with me. I surrender."

If only.

The man had no idea what he was saying and no idea what she kept dreaming about doing to him. But maybe now she'd get her chance…

CHAPTER 9

*N*ora mentally chastised herself. *What I have in store for him is a swift kick in the rear. That's it!* "Get out."

"Can I at least warm up by the fire first? It's dark out, and the roads are starting to ice over."

"Why did you drive up tonight? That was dangerous."

"You could have been hurt."

"You could have called."

He opened his mouth and closed it. "I, uh, yeah. I could have. But I wanted to see for myself that you were okay."

She waved a hand over her body. "You can see I'm fine."

"Oh yeah." He cleared his throat. "I mean, yep, you look healthy."

"So you can go back home."

"Now?" He shivered.

She didn't know if he faked it or not. Then she shivered, because damn, it was getting cold.

"I'm sorry, Nora." He did look repentant. "Mitch pretty much nagged me into setting Becca's mind at ease. She's worried about you, and he didn't want to leave her and the kids alone in that big house with the storm overhead."

"I still think you should have called." But he'd been doing a favor for Becca and Mitch. She sighed and did her best to turn off witchy-mode. "Geez. Fine. You can stay tonight. But you go home tomorrow. I mean it."

"Okay." He looked hopefully at her food. "I sure am hungry."

"Are you kidding me?"

"I brought extra food."

Her eyes narrowed. So he'd been *planning* to stay with her?

He hastened to explain, "I was shopping when Mitch called me. I didn't bring much, just enough for breakfast and maybe lunch or dinner. I usually only shop for a few days at a time."

"Hmm."

"Nora, I'm really sorry." He looked embarrassed. "I know you probably wanted to get away from everyone. I can go back home. It's not that bad out."

At that moment, wind gusted and shook the windows. Outside, trees waved through the glass, the moon bright over the flurry of snow drifting around the cabin, kicked up by high winds that showed no intention of stopping.

"It's a good hour and a half up here *without* the snow," she reminded him. "It'll take way longer than that to get back. And it's getting colder."

"Yeah. I hit some ice on the way."

"You're an idiot." With a big heart.

"An idiot who needs a grilled cheese in the worst way."

She tried not to smile. "Okay, bring in your groceries. Although you could probably leave them outside, and the cold will keep them."

"I'll bring the bag in."

He brought in *two* bags while she fixed him a sandwich and ladled him soup.

They ate in companionable silence, sharing glances before she'd quickly look away.

"So, um, I don't see a TV," Deacon said after he'd finished eating.

"It broke. My parents are replacing it with a bigger one this summer." She savored the warmth of her soup. "I brought my laptop for entertainment. And work," she said, more to herself than him.

"Huh." He took his dishes to the sink and washed them, which was a nice surprise.

When he paused by her side, she glanced up.

"Unless you're planning to lick the bowl, I'll take that."

Watching him, she deliberately licked the bowl as slowly as possible.

He only grinned.

She handed it to him, and he took her dishes to the sink and washed them too.

Nora grabbed her laptop and sat down at the dining table to type, trying to look diligent about work and not as if she had hours upon hours of streaming entertainment planned for the week. She really did have a book she wanted to write, a dream project she kept procrastinating. But part of her goal this week had been to get away and do for herself, not for everyone else in her life.

"Don't mind me," Deacon said and sat at the table next to her.

"I wasn't planning to."

He leaned around to get a better look. "What are you working on?"

She let out a loud breath and scooted so he couldn't see her screen. "My novel. Happy now?" She had to delete her next sentence which made no sense, completely off kilter. Not as if she could focus with him so close, but she was trying.

"A novel? I thought you edited articles."

She stopped attempting to type and answered him. "I do edit articles. I also do some social media marketing for local businesses in town. But my dream has always been to be a writer—of books. No better time than the present to start."

He scooted closer. "Why no better time?"

"If you move any closer, you'll be in my lap."

"Is that an invitation?" He smirked.

"*I meant* no better time as in, why not write a book now? There's no sense in waiting."

He nodded. "Right." The hunk of man-candy just sat there, watching her.

"I can't work while you're staring at me."

"Pretend I'm not here."

Her entire body was buzzing, conscious of the six-foot four mountain of muscle sitting too close.

She pushed out of her seat. "I need tea."

He stood. "I can make it."

"No. Sit." She pointed at his chair, amused despite herself when he sat back down. "And don't even *think* about reading my work. It's not done yet." She fixed herself a cup of Earl Grey, and when she turned around, she saw him reading her laptop. "Deacon. What did I just say?"

"It's good." He smiled. "Will there be sex in the story?"

She blushed and felt silly for doing so. "I don't know. Maybe."

"I can read those parts for you, no problem."

"Thanks. I think I'm good." She sat and sipped her tea, conscious of him watching her every move. "You're distracting me." She did her best to turn back to her work.

He said nothing, just watched her type until she gave up after typing the same sentence four times. She glared at him as she saved the one spelling error she'd fixed and closed her file.

"I'm sorry." He didn't seem sorry.

"Yeah, right."

"Well, not about you shutting down your work. But I am sorry I busted in on you." He brushed her hand fisted on the table. "I don't want to mess with your time off. But I'd be lying if I said I wasn't happy to see you."

Just how happy was he? She resisted the immature urge to look under the table at his crotch. *Ugh. I'm being ridiculous. And horny. And just pathetic.* Nora had no one to blame but herself. She hadn't had sex in way too long, and now a prime specimen sat next to her. The two of them all alone in a cabin that had a hot tub just out back.

She swallowed, feeling off-balanced. "Um, what do you want to do?" At his wicked grin, she hurriedly amended, "We could play a board game, watch a movie on the laptop, or hit the hot tub."

He perked up. "You have a hot tub?"

"Out back." She nodded to the back door.

"That. Definitely." He stood and froze. "I don't have a suit."

Talk about a pregnant pause.

Slowly, he added, "I suppose I could wear my underwear."

She had a hard time not envisioning that. "Um, er, sure. I guess."

"You brought a suit?"

A bikini she'd been rebellious enough to pack, considering she'd thought she'd be all alone. The one article of clothing Jenna hadn't exchanged or tucked away for her. "Yep. I'd planned on getting a good soak."

She ignored his onceover.

"I'll go take off the cover and get it running," he offered.

She forced a grin. "Sounds good."

"And Nora, seriously, I appreciate you putting up with me."

She sighed. "Yeah, yeah. Now stop telling me how wonderful I'm being before I begin to believe you."

He winked and headed outside.

After she donned her suit and grabbed two towels, she stuffed herself into her oversized terrycloth robe and prayed she'd stop imaging how she *wanted* the night to go and instead made sure she'd end it the way it *should* go. Two grown people enjoying a hot soak before going their separate ways to bed.

Emphasis on separate.

DEACON HAD TO WIPE THE SWEAT OFF HIS FOREHEAD AS IT COOLED IN the wintry weather. Jesus, what was he thinking to strip down and get close and wet with Nora Nielson? If they didn't have sex before the morning, it would be a miracle. He wanted to be with her, badly. But every time he rushed things, they inevitably went wrong.

MARIE HARTE

He grumbled under his breath and readied the hot tub, which sat partially under a massive pine, providing some cover from the icy wind. Pleased to see the water temperature a toasty 104, Deacon went back inside to quickly strip down to his underwear and tuck away his clothes, then he hurried back outside and sank up to his chin in the hot water.

"*Shit.*" He could only be glad Nora wasn't there to see him making some embarrassing faces as the sudden heat sent needles of sensation through his body, which was still struggling to make sense of the icy cold outside.

For modesty's sake, he'd left his boxer briefs on. Bubbles and the jets would help mask his arousal when it inevitably made itself visible. Just thinking about sex with Nora turned him on. Being so close to actually doing it made it all worse.

She joined him soon enough and hung up their towels on hooks near the tub. The snow continued to swirl around as if they sat in a snow globe. Mountains and a moonlit sky surrounded by clouds beyond the cabin and overlooking the lake enchanted him. Yep. He was totally going with that word, because it described the atmosphere up here.

Then Nora hung up her robe and turned to the hot tub.

His mouth dried, and he had to work to swallow past the knot in his throat.

Enchanting—that was Nora with a capital E.

She wore a skimpy two-piece that barely covered her assets, and Nora had curves that made him want to weep. She'd fit into his palms perfectly.

And there went his erection, returning full force.

She sank into the water across from him and cringed. "Oh, it's cold and hot. Prickly."

"Yep." He cleared his throat. "It's painful at first, but now I'm soaking in the heat." He casually reached over and hit the button for the bubbles and jets, needing some coverage.

She sighed. "This is great."

She sat too far away, on the opposite side of the six person tub. "Mind if I put my feet up?"

He scooted over, making use of the perpendicular seat as well. "Sounds good. I'll do the same."

They sat that way for a few minutes, each facing a different view. He had the mountains, Nora had the house. "Do you want to turn around so you can see the lake? I promise not to jump you if we sit on the same side."

She frowned at him, and he did his best not to smile. The heat stuck wisps of her brown hair to her forehead and neck, while the majority of her hair remained tucked up into an untidy bun. That and the barely-there bikini had turned her into definite fantasy material.

Nora cautiously took the seat near him, leaving a good amount of space between them. Then she stretched out, as he did, allowing the jets at her back to soothe aches and the jets near her feet to pound away her stress.

"Oh yeah. This is better."

If only she didn't sound pre-orgasmic saying that.

He swallowed a groan. "Yep. Fantastic."

The dichotomy of relaxing in the warmth while sporting a huge erection amused him. Contradictions seemed to swell when around Nora. Pun intended.

"This is nice." She closed her eyes.

He thought she looked tired. Sweet, beautiful, but fatigued, with shadows under her eyes.

MARIE HARTE

"I can feel you looking at me." She reached over to still the bubbles, leaving the jets going.

"Really?"

She opened one eye and glared at him.

"What does it feel like?" That came out way huskier than he'd intended.

Her eyes opened wide. "So we're going to go there."

"Nora?"

"Let me think a minute."

He had no idea what she needed to think about, but he needed to get a handle on his desire. So, he sat and let his mind wander, ignoring her presence, which finally had the effect he'd intended. He felt at peace, letting his worries fall away as the hot jets eased tired muscles he hadn't known he'd had.

He let out a breath and relaxed into the heat, even enjoying the bite of cold above his shoulders, and appreciated the glorious scenery of a snowy, moonlit night next to a special woman he'd come to care for, very much.

They sat in silence for some time, enough that Deacon started to feel sleepy.

"Deacon?"

"Hmm?"

"Hold this, would you?"

He obligingly held out a hand over the water, and she plopped down something wet in it. He blinked down at the fabric of a bathing suit top.

As if struck by lightning, his entire body came alive, and he shot his gaze to the tops of her breasts now bare below the water, the hint of her nudity mouthwatering.

94

"I think we should talk about the next step. Don't you?"

"The... *What?*"

"Yes, that elephant in the hot tub. And I'm not talking about the steel rod between your legs."

He just blinked at her, not sure if he was awake or dreaming.

Then she settled in his lap. Her naked breasts bobbed against him, and her silky thighs cradling him, taking the surreal situation into a *hard*, pressing reality.

"Oh God. Yes, let's talk." He draped her bikini top over the edge of the tub and planted his hands on her hips, determined to keep them there until she told him otherwise. Or he begged and she took pity on him.

Because he was closer to begging right then than when he'd first tasted Becca's sticky buns. And Deacon had one hell of a sweet tooth.

CHAPTER 10

*N*ora couldn't believe she'd done it, but she was taking charge of this weird relationship with Deacon. Talk about an early Christmas present.

"Okay, Deacon. It's like this. You and I share an attraction. Right?" She could feel it digging into her bottom.

"Oh yeah." He squeezed her hips, his gaze glued to her face.

"And it's just us up here. You and me and not a lot between us."

He glanced at her top draped over the side of the hot tub then looked back at her. "Nope."

"I haven't had sex in a while." She decided to go for blunt honesty. "I'm horny. You're here. This isn't going to be complicated. We have sex, we're nice to each other after, and that's it. We keep it between ourselves. Then you can go date half of Hope's Turn. I don't care."

He narrowed his eyes but didn't say anything. A good sign.

"I'm clean. I'm not on birth control, but it's not the right time for me to get pregnant. I don't have any condoms."

"I don't either." He looked at her lips. "I like this honesty." He shifted her, and his erection through his underwear brushed the cleft between her legs.

They both groaned, especially when her nipples dragged against his chest.

"*Fuck,*" Deacon swore, closed his eyes and took a breath, then let it out and looked at her again. "Okay, you know I've been with other women. I've dated my share, and I always, and I mean *always*, wear a condom. My ex did a number on me, and I don't ever plan to be used by a woman again."

She sighed. So much for casual sex. "Sorry, I—"

"Wait, wait." He gripped her tighter. "I just meant I'm clean. I even had a physical last month, and I'm as fit as a twenty-year old."

She just looked at him. "I thought you were thirty-nine."

His grin looked hungry. "Okay, so maybe as fit as a twenty-five-year-old. Point is, I take my health seriously. But I want inside you like you can't believe." His fingers eased on her hips and stroked her.

She felt herself melting in his arms. The snowy night, a dark prince, sex in a hot tub. All parts of a fantasy she'd been dreaming about for far too long. Reality had no place here.

"So you want to have sex with me."

"Yes, and you need to know I don't consider myself being used here. You and I are going to share hours of pleasure, Nora."

She blinked. "Hours?"

His naughty grin sent her pulse racing. "Oh yeah. But the first time is going to be fast. I've been dreaming about you for a long time. And you have me ready to go off. I have to see you. But hold on." He shifted her and wriggled out of his underwear, tossing them next to her bikini top. Then he took the bottoms she handed him and set them aside.

He lifted her up so that her breasts broke the water, her nipples stiff from the cold and an arousal she couldn't hide.

"So pretty." He leaned forward to lick water off her nipples, and she sighed and clasped his head to her, consciously straddling his body and tucking the head of his shaft inside her. He stilled and pulled his mouth away, his eyes so dark they looked black. "Nora, are you sure?"

"About my life? Not at all. About this? You and me?" She smiled, and her expression must have cemented the deal, because he dragged her down, filling her one inch at a time as his thick cock pushed through her flesh until they had joined as tightly as two people could be.

"*Yes,*" she hissed and kissed him.

He kissed her back, moaning into her mouth, and guided her to ride him.

She moved, loving how full she felt, and nipped his lower lip when his large palms caressed her breasts.

"That's it, baby. Yeah," he murmured and flicked her nipples. "You are so fucking beautiful."

The sex was all-consuming. Deacon not only had an amazing body, he took the time to make her feel pleasure. And the words. *Yes, please,* he used the words. Called her beautiful. Told her how much he wanted to fill her up. How he could think of no one but her all the time.

He delivered the fantasy, along with an orgasm that crashed into her the moment he put a thick finger between her legs to rub her with a finesse she hadn't known a man could have.

She cried out and slammed harder onto him, and he lost it.

He held her down, groaning her name as he came. Water sloshed everywhere as Deacon hugged her to him, his face pressed against her shoulder while he jetted into her with that rock-hard body.

She stroked his shoulders, his nape, and toyed with the wet strands of hair against his neck.

When he finally ceased, he relaxed his hold around her middle and sat them both back, deeper into the water. He blinked at her, and she didn't know what to think.

He didn't make a joke or smile. Instead, he cupped her cheek and drew her close for a kiss that promised tenderness and affection.

When he pulled away, the smile he gave her was both happy and what looked almost loving. "That was out of this world."

She nodded, not able to speak past the lump in her throat. A ball of emotion had no place between them considering her warnings about keeping things casual. What the hell had just happened?

"I'm sorry."

She gaped. "Sorry? For what?"

"For going too fast." He sighed and dragged those magic hands up her body to cup her breasts. "When we're done in here, I have some work to do in the bedroom."

"Huh?"

The familiar grin she knew and *used to* loathe appeared. "Oh ho, so I've finally made you speechless. Good to know an orgasm will do that."

"Oh stop." She blushed and realized her remained inside her, still thick and solid. "You're still hard?"

"I'm always hard around you," he admitted. "Just give it a little bit. It'll go down, I promise."

She snorted. "Not exactly what a girl likes to hear." To her surprise, she wanted him again. "So you're saying you can do better when dry and in a bed?"

"The key points being *me* dry and in a bed. You, sweetheart, need to stay nice and wet." He caressed her breasts, which had her squirming on his lap. "Unless you want to get me there sooner." He sighed. "Nora, you have the nicest tits."

"Nice language."

He chuckled and slipped out of her. "Oh, damn."

She paused. "We had sex in the family hot tub. I'm going to hell for sure."

He laughed harder. "Don't worry. With the chemicals cleaning contaminates and the temperature, my little swimmers will die off soon enough." He pulled her close to nuzzle her neck and said into her ear, "But think about what I left inside of you. It's turning me on, baby. Coming in you. Just let me know when you're ready for round two."

She shivered, still in lust with the aggravatingly sexy man. "I'm always good to go. It's you manly types who need time to recover."

He stretched, and she couldn't help glancing at all those muscles expanding and contracting.

"You know, I'm getting cheated. I haven't seen you naked yet."

He grinned and pulled her up against him, hugging her to his warm body.

Nora felt the closeness deep inside and sighed, enjoying this short reprieve from loneliness.

"Trust me. You'll faint at the sight of my huge—"

"Deacon."

"Legs. Huge thighs, I was going for." He snickered. "What did you think I was going to say?" He kissed her. "I can't believe you, the same woman who took off her top and straddled me, is embarrassed by some frank talk."

"I'm not embarrassed."

"No?" His frown of concentration turned to a large grin. "Oh, I see. Not embarrassed. Turned on by some dirty talk, are we?"

"Maybe," she admitted.

"Fuck. Me too." He squeezed her shoulder. "We have a lot more in common than I thought." Before she could say anything, he interrupted with, "I know, I know. This is just casual. It's just sex. But Nora, we can have fun with it. I swear I won't ruin things the way I always seem to with you."

"You mean by disappearing without a word?"

He groaned. "I made a mistake. I admit it. I was wrong. You were right."

"You were scared." She felt cocky and entitled to the feeling, all things considered.

"Maybe."

"Maybe?"

"Fine. I was scared," he muttered. "But you're intimidating."

She laughed. "I'm a good hundred pounds less than you and nearly a foot shorter. How scary can I be?"

He shuddered. "Scarier than Krampus. Trust me on that."

They sat in the hot tub for a while longer, eventually parting to get the jets on their bodies, relieving any aches.

Every time they made eye contact, Deacon smiled at her. And Nora smiled back, wondering if the sex had changed everything, or if the physical pleasure had muted her feelings of isolation and allowed her to be at ease.

"Deacon? I'm glad you came."

He paused then said with all seriousness, "I am too."

Nora couldn't tell if he'd caught the double-entendre or meant he was happy to be with her up here in the mountains.

But she didn't want to know, so she didn't ask. Because it didn't matter. What they had was merely sexual.

DEACON DRIED OFF AND JOINED NORA IN HER BEDROOM, STOKING UP the fire in the room while she towel-dried the wet parts of her hair. She'd let the bun out, and her long brown hair feathered over her shoulders and breasts, framing a face he'd committed to memory.

The sex had killed any rebellious brain cells surviving his orgasm. He had to have her again, to prove he could drive her wild, so that the stubborn woman would rethink her plan to keep their relationship casual.

Granted, he didn't want marriage and babies tomorrow. But his fear of commitment, when around Nora, shifted into something else. A longing for togetherness, to hold her hand and watch her smile. Yes, the sex was fucking amazing. But feeling her pleasure had showed him how much her joy mattered, more so than his own.

How long had it been since he'd been so sincere in wanting the best for someone else? Had he been so wrapped in self-pity and loathing for connivers that he'd put every woman he dated in the role of villain from the get-go?

"You okay?" Nora stared at him, her gaze bringing him easily back to a state of pleasurable arousal.

"Oh, yeah." He grinned, loving the way her eyes widened as he thickened under her stare. "Nora, my eyes are up here," he teased.

She flushed. "I can't help it. You're huge."

"Yes, I am." He smothered the smirk that threatened.

She rolled her eyes but laughed. "Okay, you're hung like a dinosaur, you're that big."

"Well, if you say so." He walked towards her. "You sure you're okay with me coming inside you? Because I plan on doing that a lot tonight."

She nodded and let him tug her to him. "I liked it. A lot. I know my body, and it's not the right time to get pregnant." The word seemed to hover between them. "But you never know when something might happen."

She watched him. He watched her back. "I like kids."

"So do I," she said slowly. "I kind of want my own."

"Me too." He kissed her, because he had to. "I want to get married—to the right woman—and have a bunch."

She nodded and kissed him back, and his hands seemed to move of their own volition and slid beneath her robe to mold her plump breasts. "I want a lot of kids."

The kid talk should have scared him straight the hell out of there. Instead, it made him harder. Need swamped him, the desire to fill Nora again making it impossible to resist her. "Hmm." He lifted her in his arms, shocking a gasp out of her. "Let's get you naked and on the bed."

She nodded, watching him with wide eyes.

The dark brown of her irises sucked him in, pulling at him to sate her desire—for him. "Fuck, Nora. I need you." He meant every word, and in more ways than one.

As he set her on the bed and stripped off her robe, he saw a beautiful, naked woman looking up at him with a vulnerability she wouldn't like to know she'd shared. A need to protect her had him taking more care, tempering his fierce desire.

He crawled over her body, kissing her shoulders, her chest, her neck. He kept his weight on his elbows while he brushed against her soft body with his harder one. She felt amazing against his sensitive skin, her femininity a drug addicting him kiss by kiss.

Deacon kissed her soft lips, sliding his tongue inside her and tasting the passion he craved.

She wound her arms around his neck and tugged him closer, darting her tongue against his while she slid her thighs on either side of his hips, putting herself in very close contact with that part of him that refused to go down.

He needed to pull back before he slid inside her and kept on pumping until they both came, so he reluctantly broke from the kiss.

"We need to slow down," he rasped and kissed his way to her breasts. The berry-red nipples begged for his teeth, and knowing how much his touch turned her on had him focusing there for some time.

"Deacon, fuck me," she whispered, pulling at his shoulders. "In me. Come on."

"Not yet." He cupped her breasts and sucked harder, making her arch up into him. Then he moved down her body, kissing his way to her warm, wet center.

"Deacon, oh God."

He kissed her clit and slid a finger inside her, thrilled to find evidence of her passion. "Baby, you're so wet. So sweet." He licked her while fucking her with his finger, and when she cried out and came, he continued to pull at her tender flesh.

She ground against his mouth. "Again."

He smiled and kissed her inner thighs, loving how Nora owned her sexuality. He wanted the dynamo even more.

"This time it's my turn." Nora moved out from under him, her dark eyes shining, her body quivering with spent pleasure. "On your back, big guy. And scoot down." She tossed the pillows to the side.

He did as she asked. Then he watched her crawl up his body and kneel on either side of his neck. He anticipated her taste and gripped her thighs. "Oh yeah."

"I want to feel your tongue inside me. I want to feel those teeth on my clit."

He gripped his throbbing erection, knowing he was close. The sensual promise in her eyes snared him. "Yes." He let her kneel over him and gave her what she wanted, her cries for more egging him on.

He moaned, loving everything about this moment.

Then the blasted woman stopped him.

"You didn't come yet," he complained, out of breath, and wiped his lips with his hand, loving her body.

"Not without you," she said coyly and turned around.

Deacon's entire body tensed. "Nora, honey, I'm really close."

"And I'm a good girl who knows how to swallow. So get crackin'." She laughed and leaned forward.

The hot breath on his cock had him getting as close to her as he could. He kissed and licked her, and she ground her pussy against his mouth, even harder when he thrust a thick finger inside her, giving her what she needed. He drew her clit into his mouth and sucked her into an orgasm that quickly set off his own.

As Nora climaxed, she tightened her mouth over him and bobbed faster, her hands cupping his tight balls. Deacon lost his mind. He gave her one last kiss and pushed her up off him, but Nora didn't stop sucking. He exploded into her mouth, completely done in.

She moved her lower body to kneel next to him while she continued to swallow him down.

When he finally stopped, barely able to function, she kissed her way up his body and joined him in bed, laying her head on his shoulder.

"Jesus, Nora." Deacon blinked up at the ceiling, dizzy.

She chuckled. "Wow, Deacon. Pent up, were we? I think I nearly drowned."

He flushed. "Stop."

She laughed harder and snuggled into him.

He sighed, feeling the rightness of it all, wishing he could go to bed every night like this, with Nora by his side, done in after sharing their bodies and minds.

And he fell asleep, dreaming of a future that put a smile on his face.

CHAPTER 11

*N*ora woke the next morning confused. At first.

She lay on her side, cuddled against an inferno. A thick arm had wrapped around her middle, a hand on the flat of her stomach, keeping her glued to the fiery body plastered against her back.

Deacon. Flashman. She'd had sex with the quarterback, and he'd nailed every play. Good Lord.

She felt her cheeks heat.

"Nora?" came the husky question.

"Hmm?"

"Yeah." He sighed into the crook of her neck, edged his thigh between her legs to spread her for him, and pushed into her.

The morning quickie brought her to a surprising orgasm in no time, followed by Deacon's hoarse moan as he emptied inside her.

Considering what a stickler she'd always been for safe sex, that she'd had unprotected sex with Deacon all night long and now this morning

MARIE HARTE

should have panicked her. Instead, she felt better than good. She felt amazing.

She stretched and reached for the towel they'd been using to keep the sheets from getting messy.

After using it, she left the bed to shower. When he made a move to enter behind her, she stopped him at the door. "Nope. You need to wait. The other bathroom is down the hall if you need it."

He looked down at her with an imposing glare then stomped away without a word.

Victorious in her need for morning autonomy, she took a quick shower, getting clean, and refused to worry that she wasn't worrying. Normal Nora would rethink her decisions and question herself to death. Fantasy/Christmas Nora loved everything about her time at the cabin. Period.

After drying off, she dressed in her least tight shirt, foregoing a bra because it was her week of vacation after all, and ignored tight jeans in favor of the lounge pants she'd been wearing the previous day.

A sexy, naked Deacon passed by her in the hallway with a grunt and shut himself in the bathroom. She heard the shower go on and grinned. So, Deacon was officially not a morning person.

Good to know.

No, not good to know. She sighed. *This is why I never should have had sex with Deacon. Because now I'm acting like there will be a tomorrow with the guy, and we just had sex.*

That's it.

Sex. Amazing, unforgettable, best-sex-of-my-entire-life sex. Hell, we even had glorious quickie morning sex that gave me a jaw-dropping orgasm. Don't overthink. Remember, this is your Christmas present to yourself. Indulge and enjoy.

She started a pot of coffee then decided to fry up some bacon and eggs, making enough for Deacon before he headed back down the mountain.

At the thought, her happy mood fizzled.

Deacon joined her, wearing the jeans and sweater he'd worn yesterday. He studied her carefully. "Good morning."

"Yeah, yeah." She waved the spatula around. "You want eggs or what?"

His wariness faded, replaced by amusement. "So, maybe I'm not the only non-morning person around."

"I like my mornings with coffee. Usually." She nodded to the snow outside. "I guess you'll be heading back." She whipped her head back to the window, what she was seeing finally registering. "Or not."

They both approached the front bay window and stared at his vehicle halfway covered in snow.

He turned a shocked look her way. "That's more than a few inches out there. And it's still snowing." His lips curled into a grin. "I guess I should check the weather, because, I mean, it might not be safe to drive back yet."

She responded in a smile, a lightness making her world right again. "You know, you should. With all that snow, it can't be safe heading back yet."

They grinned at each other, but Nora was grateful Deacon didn't mention why they seemed so happy about not parting ways. It felt odd to want to be with him so much. She knew the sex had been off-the-charts hot, but just sitting with him felt good. Too good.

She shut down any warnings going off in her mind and offered him some coffee before getting back to fixing breakfast.

"I'll get it, thanks." Deacon helped himself and closed his eyes. "This is really good."

"From the local beanery near Bragg's Tea."

He opened his eyes. "I love those guys." He watched her cook and stared at the food she piled up on two plates. "Which one is mine?"

"The big one."

He blinked. "They're both piled with bacon and eggs."

She huffed. "No they're not. Mine is smaller. See?" She took the clearly smaller plate of food.

He chuckled. "If you say so."

"I do."

"Right. But hey, you earned that big meal. Got to make up for burning so many calories last night." He paused. "And this morning."

She refused to look at him until they finished breakfast.

Once again, he did the dishes without being asked.

"Did your mom train you to be so well-behaved?"

"She tried." He shot her a grin over his shoulder. "Some of it took, like the dishes. But I'm not a fan of laundry. And I try, but I'm not a great cook."

"I've heard." She refreshed her coffee and watched him, coming to the realization she liked watching him work, liked having someone to talk to in the morning, and that it wasn't just any body she liked, but Deacon in particular.

He fetched his phone and returned with a frown. "It might be a few days before I can head back. Look at the mountain conditions and forecast."

He handed her his phone, and she read the bad news. That wasn't so bad.

"I guess it's a good thing you have groceries."

"Wish I had some extra clothes." He paused. "Let me go check my SUV. Sometimes I leave a gym bag with stuff in it." Deacon left and returned wearing a frown and carrying a large duffel bag—not a small gym bag. "I didn't pack this or put it in my trunk. My gym bag is a lot smaller."

"Oh?"

His eyes narrowed. "I was, however, visited by Simon before I left to check on you."

Nora frowned. "I thought you were grocery shopping and got the call from Mitch?"

"That's true. But before that I was at home, and Simon came by to visit." He put the bag down and looked through it then sighed. He pulled a handful of condoms out of the bag. "This isn't exactly how I'd pack for a night out. And for the record, I don't think I could use this many condoms in a week." He paused. "Well, maybe a really good week."

She wondered... "You know, Jenna visited me before I left for the cabin. And I unpacked a bag full of lingerie, thongs, and tight clothes." She plucked at her sweater, saw him follow the movement. "I'd packed pajamas and comfy clothes."

"Well, Jenna has good taste in sweaters." Deacon winked. "That bikini last night near about gave me a heart attack. And when it came off..."

Nora grinned. "The bikini was all me. I didn't think anyone would be around to see me wearing it though."

"I will never forget it."

She laughed. "I've never worn it in public before. It's indecent."

"I know. And like I said, it's ingrained into my brain, never to be forgotten."

"Yeah, well, your suit was better than mine." She wiggled her brows.

"Well, I'll be wearing it in the hot tub while I'm here, so get used to it."

"I'll try, but it's *hard* to get used to." She laughed at the face he made.

"That was terrible."

"I know." She gave him a smug smile that faded as he stared from his clothes to her. "What's wrong?"

He sighed. "I want to have more sex. A lot more sex. I also don't want to keep you from your much earned vacation. Roy can handle work while I'm gone. But I realized I have nothing to do but bother you. And I don't want you bothered… Well, not unless you're hot and bothered."

"Now *that* was terrible."

He didn't laugh with her. "Is it terrible I'm here? Be honest."

"No." She sighed. "It should be awful. I came up here to get away from everyone. But last night was more fun than I've had in a long, long time. And I'm kind of glad not to be alone, if you want the truth."

His expression softened. "So am I. It's so easy to be in a crowd and feel like you're the only one there, isn't it?"

She nodded.

He walked to her and gave her a huge hug. Then a kiss that turned hot way too fast. He pulled back and had to catch his breath. "You do that to me. Every time."

"Yeah, me too." She shook her head, hoping to clear the lust from her brain. "I did want to get some writing done."

He pulled back. "I can keep myself busy while you're working. But maybe when you're done, we could spend time together." At her look, he flushed. "Not just fucking. Er, having sex."

She bit back a grin, liking his discomfort. Deacon always acted smug or self-assured. Seeing this part of him, the real man behind the handsome face, made her treasure their time together as authentic. Something she didn't think he shared with many people outside his close friends and family.

She winked. "Fucking is fine too."

He laughed. "What about making love? Can we do that later?"

"As opposed to fucking? Isn't it the same thing?"

He rolled his eyes. "Where is the romantic in you? Fucking is animal sex. Making love uses gaga eyes and smoochy words." He pursed his lips and made moony-eyed faces at her that had her laughing hysterically.

Who knew Deacon could be so funny?

She wiped her eyes, still laughing. "That's *it*. As soon as I get done working on this section, you and I are settling in for an afternoon of popcorn and Christmas movies. I downloaded both Hallmark and Lifetime. You're welcome."

"Shoot me now."

DEACON HAD NEVER FELT SO AT EASE WITH A WOMAN. HE SAT ON THE couch and read a book—a romance book on Nora's e-reader she'd recommended—and got both turned on and entertained. He wanted to recreate the sex scene with Nora later.

While he read and kept quiet, she worked on the dining table typing and scribbling in her notebook every so often.

As promised, when finished, she forced him to watch Christmas movies. In the three they watched back-to-back (not as terrible as he'd feared the experience to be), the leading man wore plaid and came from a small town. The woman, a city dweller, left her citified fiancé/boyfriend for the small town plaid guy and moved in with him to start a pumpkin patch, a Christmas tree farm, and in the last instance, a lavender farm. The real shocker—Nora cried at the happy endings.

After their last movie ended, he held a tissue for her. "Is that what you want? Some small town farmer to sweep you off your feet and plant flowers?"

"Hush. It was wonderful."

"Hmm."

"What does that mean?"

"It means you're a romantic. Under the snarls, the snark, and the fuckery, you like a good romance."

"So what? And what's wrong with fuckery?"

He had to smile. Nora always cursed with such flair. "Nothing. So if I give you a candlelit dinner, chocolates, and flowers, you'd be happy with that?" Wait, he hadn't meant to ask her straight out what she liked.

"Well, duh." She blinked. "But you and I are just in this for sex, right? It's simple. We shouldn't complicate it."

"Of course." Yet he needed to know more. "But if, for the sake of argument, a guy wanted to date you, that's what you'd like? Romance?" Bundles of lavender?

"I guess. If he meant it. It's nice when you're in that new dating phase where you try to impress each other. But at some point, you need to be honest about what you like. Forcing a nonromantic guy to be romantic never works. Trust me. I know."

"I like football, but my girlfriend wouldn't have to love it."

"I like books, but my boyfriend wouldn't have to read them."

"That one I was reading earlier was pretty good. I liked it."

She didn't tease him for admitting the truth but agreed instead. "Me too."

"Is that what you're trying to write?"

"Yes, kind of. More of a fiction than a romance, or what they call women's fiction, which is actually just fiction, but for some reason it's labeled as *women's* fiction." She sneered. "As if women are less legitimate than... Why are you looking at me like that?"

"You're cute when you ramble."

"Shut up."

He laughed then asked a question he hadn't intended. "Do *you* like football?"

"I, well, yes. I mean, I like to watch the players in their tight pants." She grinned at him. "When Simon started playing, I took more interest in it. Then Becca got involved with Mitch, and I figured it wouldn't hurt to learn the sport." She eyed him up and down. "You have to be pretty smart to be a quarterback."

He waited for the snippy comment sure to follow, surprised when it didn't. "Er, yeah. Lots of plays to know, the ability to read the field. And it depends on the coach and how much faith he has in you to run the offense. Some coaches are more hands-on. Mine wasn't."

"You missed winning a Super Bowl twice. And you won team MVP five years out of the seven you played. You were at the top of your game."

His eyes widened. He hadn't realized she knew that much about his sports career.

Seeing his surprise, she blushed and mumbled, "Mitch talks about you sometimes."

He felt warm that she cared enough to remember that much. "I loved the game. No question." He had to tread carefully now, aware he'd screwed up with her in the past when moving too fast. "But it's over. I have a life I really like right now. Great friends, great family, a hot woman who gets even hotter when she's wet."

"*Deacon.*"

"I meant in the hot tub. That kind of wet. Geez, Nora. Get your head out of the gutter."

She laughed at him. "Nice try."

"I like this." He smiled. "Us being friends. Laughing and talking. You not mad at me."

She sobered, looking him over carefully, and added, "And fucking like rabbits."

"Well, of course. I didn't think that needed to be said."

She seemed to relax, which he found curious. It was almost as if she'd rather chalk up their relationship to the nothing but the physical, letting it mean less than it did. Than it should.

Fuck. What *did* their relationship, such as it was, mean exactly?

"Deacon, about us together…" Nora paused.

Instead of cutting in and making a hash of things, he waited.

She finished with, "I think it's nice too."

That was it? Just nice? Well, he'd take what he could get. For now. Because being with Nora had opened him up to some possibilities, thoughts and feelings for a woman he hadn't had in a long time. The warmth in his chest scared and excited him. But he'd take it slow. Look for the long game.

And if he had a shot at winning this particular title, he'd need to employ strategy.

"Good. I think so too." He leaned close to kiss her on the cheek. "But if I have to watch one more man in plaid fold under mistletoe, I might puke. How about we play some games after a quick break?"

"Fine. But I play to win."

"So do I."

They shared evil grins.

"Winner does dishes and gives backrubs," Deacon challenged.

"Oh, you're on. And foot rubs too. Don't forget those."

He raised his size thirteen feet in socks with no holes, thank goodness, and wiggled his toes. "Bring it, Nielson."

"Back at ya, Flashman."

They broke even at two to two. But Deacon considered all things equal since they ended in bed.

And Nora's rubs gave all new meaning to feeling good.

CHAPTER 12

*E*arly Friday afternoon, Nora watched the snow start to recede. The weather hadn't overly warmed, but the sky was bright, and the sun had melted enough snow that Deacon could at least get to his vehicle without being knee-deep in the stuff.

For two days, she and Deacon had played games, watched movies, eaten bad-for-you food, and followed up with even worse wine—the cheap and sweet stuff that didn't strain Nora's budget. And they had sex. Glorious, orgasmic, heart-stopping sex that continued to push at Nora's emotional boundaries.

Deacon always saw to her needs first. He seemed to love watching her enjoy herself, and with him, she never felt self-conscious for letting go. He made her feel beautiful, and he liked to cuddle and talk after they lay together, giving her a warm feeling inside. That maybe, like her, he felt more than just physical pleasure from their joining. But that they clicked on other levels too.

She smothered a sigh and shot him a side glance, content just to watch him. He hadn't shaved, and though the scratchy feel of his cheeks against her skin wasn't the nicest, it could be disturbingly sexy when rubbed against the right places. Plus, he looked like some kind of bad boy biker/tough guy. Straight out of one of her books.

It had surprised her, and him, if she read him correctly, to find he enjoyed her fictional taste. Granted, he kept wanting them to act out the sex scenes, but he also liked talking to her about the intricate plots.

With any luck, she'd continue to write her own book and eventually finish it before she turned forty.

She grimaced, realizing her birthday—the big *three-five*—loomed close. Just eleven more days to Christmas Eve and her being that much further from having a family of her own. She stared without seeing at the snow outside.

"What's with the depressed look?" Deacon asked.

Startled, she jumped and snapped, "Do you have eyes in the back of your head?"

"Yep. Wanna see?" He rubbed his head. "Ow, just poked myself in the eye."

Nora tried not to smile, but she loved the fact Deacon could dish out the sarcasm as well as take it. "I'm not depressed. Well, a little. I want to go outside and enjoy the weather, but I should be writing."

He put the e-reader down and joined her by the front window. "Wow. It's beautiful out there. Put on your boots and coat. We can go for a walk." He started to head for the closet and slowed. "Or is this your way of asking me to head back?" He pasted a smile on that didn't look sincere. And that made her happy. Deacon didn't want to leave. "I should probably check the weather—"

"Don't bother," she interrupted before letting out a loud, put-upon breath. "You might as well stay the weekend. I mean, to make sure it's really clear before you head back to town. And with all the weekend traffic you're sure to hit even going down the mountain, it'll be safer to wait until the crowds clear. Unless you need to get back to make up for missed work?"

He'd been borrowing her computer at night to catch up on emails and some business, but he hadn't seemed stressed about missing the job.

"No, I'm good. Letting me use your laptop has helped." Deacon visibly relaxed. "That's a good point about traffic. It would be better if I could finish out the weekend here." Neither mentioned beating the traffic back *down* the mountain before the weekend skiers. The better bet would be for him to leave today, honestly.

"Yeah, that's a good plan." She tried to play it off. "I'm leaving Monday morning. You could always leave with me."

"Sounds good." He crossed to her side and gave her a hug and a kiss.

The man loved to cuddle, and every time he took her in his arms, she felt both cared for and safe. She didn't understand how his ex-wife had ever thought she might want someone else. Then again, the man *had* ghosted Nora after their one and only date.

Nora had a tough time remembering that when being kissed by the giant ball of sex appeal in her arms.

They put on their boots and winter gear and headed outside for a walk. Still deep in spots, the snow was more than manageable for Deacon, while Nora had to take smaller, slower steps.

"Hold on, Deacon. Not all of us are six-eleven."

"Six-four. But what, you're on the small side of five feet, right?"

"Jerk. I'm five-seven. I'm tall."

"You keep thinking that." He waited for her to catch up then reached for her hand and held onto it while they walked through the snow.

The sun shone overhead, making the snow glisten, the bright white almost glaringly painful in certain spots. "I should have brought sunglasses."

"Me too."

They walked side by side, and Nora felt the familiar weight of worry and stress gone from her shoulders. "I love being out in the sun."

"I don't get out enough. I know that, but it always seems like I have so much other stuff to do." He stopped her and pointed up at the sky.

They watched as an eagle soared overhead, its majesty breathtaking set against the backdrop of snowcapped mountains and white powdered pines. The air smelled crisp and of evergreens, and Nora clutched the large hand in her own, her heart thundering, racing toward a scary feeling she had no right to.

But when she would have pulled her hand away, Deacon wouldn't let her.

"Stop. We're having a moment," he insisted. "We saw an eagle. That's magical. Don't ruin it with your petty human complaints."

She blinked up at him. "What?"

"Sorry. That was in the book I was reading. Did you know that women think shapeshifters are sexy?"

"Um, yes. I did know that." Random change of topic, but she'd go with it. She also left her hand in his, unable to admit to herself how much she cherished being with Deacon, having him all to herself.

"If you were a shapeshifter, I'd peg you as a bird of some kind. An eagle or an owl."

"Oh, thanks." She warmed. "Why a bird?"

"A bird of prey," he corrected. "Because you're sharp and savage."

"Thanks a lot."

"But so pretty everyone stops and watches when you pass by." He winked.

"Oh, that was good."

"I try."

She grinned.

"What about me? What kind of animal would I be?"

"Hmm." She watched him as the walked. "A bear."

His mouth turned down. "Not a wolf or a tiger?"

"Nah. You lumber. You're not sleek. You're too big and muscular."

He perked up. "Oh, sure. I'm too powerful and strong for a mere wolf."
He flexed with his free arm. "Check me out."

"Stop." But she did try to feel his biceps through the coat and her
mitten. "Oooh, I'm so impressed."

He grunted. "You're damned right."

They teased and continued their magical trek through the snow on a
path she remembered toward the lake. Nora kept them close between
the trees, conscious of the danger to be had when snow covered the
ground, hiding divots and sometimes tree wells. Just last year they'd
lost a skier to one, and it had been a tragic accident that might have
been avoided.

"Deacon, can I ask you a question?" she said before she could change
her mind.

"Sure."

*No, that's too intimate for this thing between you and me. Leave it
alone.* Smart Nora had the best advice. Except risk-taker Nora spoke
before she could censor herself. "Why did you and Rhonda break up? I
know it's not my business, but I just can't figure it out." She glanced
up him with curiosity. "I mean, you don't have to tell me, but…"

"But you'll hound me until you know?" he asked, his smile apparent
though she noted a flicker of sadness in his eyes.

They stopped walking at the edge of the lake, where a wooden deck extended into the frozen water. There they mutually parted hands, watching each other and the lake, which seemed to move as the loose snow covering the ice shifted with a gentle wind.

"Do you miss her?"

"Rhonda? Hell no." His adamant refusal relieved her. "I miss what I thought we had. And I wish she hadn't done what she did to me. She's the reason I have a lot of trust issues." He sighed. "I'm not blameless in our relationship failing, but I always tried to treat her with respect. Until the end, then... I just wanted her gone."

Nora had no right to pry into his private life. She started to feel bad, not wanting to ruin the magical moments they had left of their time at the cabin. But for some reason, it had felt okay to speak up. "I'm sorry I asked."

"No, you're not."

"No, I'm not."

He gave her a real smile. "That's what I like about you, Nora. You're honest. Sometimes to a fault, but I know where I stand with you."

I wish I could say the same, but I have no idea what our relationship is. She cleared her throat. "Well?"

"Fine. I'll tell you all the gory details." His eyes narrowed. "Then I get to pry into your personal life."

"I have nothing to hide." Sadly, she didn't.

"Okay, the whole story... You sure you want to hear this?" At her nod, he continued. "I was a star in the pros. I knew I was good. I had women throwing themselves at me. Not to sound conceited, but that's kind of how it goes when you make the draft and go from backup quarterback to starting in a year. Plus, I'd never had a problem with women, even back in high school."

She frowned. "You wouldn't."

He sighed. "It's not as great as it sounds. In school, I was popular with sports and grades, and the girls liked me. But I used to wonder if they'd like me if I hadn't captained the football or basketball teams."

"Wait. Basketball too?"

"I was great at baseball as well, but I tried to use the spring season to focus on football."

"Geez. I was president of the debate club and played a few seasons of lacrosse, but nothing serious."

He smiled. "I can totally see you as the debate queen."

She fake-fluffed her hat-covered hair. "I'll take queen. More like debate dictator, but queen sounds nicer." She liked that he relaxed more, because she knew the subject of his marriage still hurt.

"Anyway, I dated my share. But I was always honest, not a player or a cheat. I was so devoted to my career that dating took a backseat to the game. Then a few friends married, and I thought it was time for me to get serious about more than football. Rhonda seemed nice, not too into me, so I had to work harder to get her." He made a face. "I know that sounds terrible. But playing hard to get works sometimes."

"Until you get what you thought you wanted, and it's not all it's cracked up to be."

"You got that right." He shoved his hands in his pockets and faced the water, looking off into the distance. "We dated for a year, and she continued to model, so she wasn't always around. I ignored the caution at the back of my mind, telling myself that her coolness was just a part of her. That she loved my support that let her quit her job and stay home. That she loved me for more than the presents and the trips and the lavish lifestyle."

She didn't speak, feeling compassion for a man who'd wanted more.

"I'm not a homebody like Mitch. I liked the parties and the wild life at first. But then I just wanted to spend time with my wife. I wanted kids." He shook his head. "I married her and hurt my arm soon after. That injury was a disaster." He rotated his right shoulder and winced. "It still gives me problems when it's cold. But what really killed me was having to leave the game. I thought I had Rhonda, my friends, family. I didn't."

She tugged his jacket. "Deacon, you don't have to say anymore."

"No, I want to tell you." He turned and looked at her. "Rhonda pulled away. I was miserable, and maybe I didn't pay her enough attention. Maybe I held onto the hope I'd return to the game too long. But she was cheating on me, and it hurt. I had my pride, you know? I ignored the tabloids and the rumors for a while. I started drinking to ignore everything. I had so much still going for me, but I couldn't see it.

"I turned down opportunities for sponsorships and broadcasting after my injury, because if I couldn't play the game, why bother?"

"Ouch."

"Yeah, I was really lost for a while. Then it got worse, because when Rhonda found out I'd deliberately turned away money, she flaunted her affairs—plural. Then she filed for divorce, I guess to shock me. When I agreed, she grew livid."

"What? You were supposed to stay with her while she screwed around on you?" Incensed on his behalf, Nora glared. "What a bitch."

"That's what Mitch said." He gave a ghost of a smile. "My mom too. Oh man, you should have heard her go off on Rhonda." Deacon sighed. "It took three years for the divorce to go through. And I was a basket case. I refused therapy, because the physical therapy wasn't helping the way I thought it should, and the mental stuff was for people who needed it. Not me." He snorted. "Hell, I was lying to everyone. I kept partying and drinking, hanging out with people who used me for anything they could. I didn't tell my family how bad I felt. And I..." He cleared his throat. "I wasn't in a good place. Roy kept nagging me to visit him, to get away from it all."

"So you came here, to Hope's Turn."

"I was at the end of my rope. My attorneys were great but costing me a ton. Then I found out I had to pay for Rhonda's debts—and we're talking in the millions of dollars, here."

"Holy shit."

He nodded. "The only good thing to come from her leaving was that she quickly hooked up with another player and wanted to get married. So I got off, I guess you could say, with no spousal support. Just the millions to pay for her mansion, jewelry, and lifestyle." He shrugged. "I finally had a clean break and no life worth living." He quickly added, "Or so I thought. Mitch and my parents didn't know how bad I was, mentally, until I was on the road to recovery thanks to Roy. And thanks to Hope's Turn."

He smiled down at her, and something inside her melted, reaching out to him. "This town healed me. It let me feel like I was worth something again, you know?"

She nodded.

"But it took a while living here before I felt comfortable to go out and date again. Nora, believe it or not, I went for nearly two years without having sex with anyone."

"Seriously?" She gaped. "But you're so..."

"Sexual? Yeah. Rhonda fucked me up," he said bluntly.

"Wow. She sure did."

"Then I made some friends. Nothing serious, but we'd hook up, and I felt better about women. But I was seriously hating for a while. It wasn't right, and I felt bad about being so angry, but I couldn't help it."

"You really hated women?" She thought about it. "Although, I understand. I've gone through more than a few man-hating phases. Guys can be dogs."

"Yeah, well so can women."

She nodded. "I hear you."

"Uh-huh." He blew out a breath. "Anyway, I'm on the mend, and then my little brother blows into town. Women are all over the guy. And that spills over to me."

"And then he meets Becca."

Deacon smiled, and the expression turned him from handsome to beautiful, the joy in his eyes lighting up his face. "He fell in love. When the great Flash was off the market, women started looking at me."

"So you dated the entire town of Hope's Turn." She nodded, still nursing the bit of hurt that he'd blown her off.

"Not *all* of the town," he said. "The one woman who made me sweaty and nervous as hell seemed not to like me much. Then she kept trying to get me to help her trick my brother into dating Becca."

Me. He means I made him sweaty and nervous. "Wait. What?"

He nodded. "I've thought about it a lot. That date we had. It was great. And I got…"

"Scared?"

"Not exactly. More like—"

"Terrified? Shaken? Knocked on your ass?"

He frowned. "No. More like I was uneasy."

She snorted. "Scared."

"Who is telling this story?"

"Fine, fine." She waved him to continue. "Go on."

He continued to frown. "After our date, I left for business and let myself forget about you for a little while. My life was easy, fun. Not

127

filled with angst or nerves. And so, well, maybe I wasn't as nice to you as I should have been."

Nora, not the most delicate of listeners, poked him in the chest. "*Maybe?*"

"Fuck. Okay, I'm sorry! I was a dick, and I was scared," he growled. "Happy now?"

"Actually…yes."

He blinked. "Really?"

CHAPTER 13

*R*eally? Deacon had laid his heart on the line for her, telling her the truth about being a huge loser and how terrible his life choices had been, and she was glad to hear it? Was he still that bad a judge of character?

"I'm happy you finally gave me a sincere apology," Nora explained, looking way too cute in her red hat and coat with those snowflake mittens and matching boots. "I knew I'd scared you."

"Oh, is that right?" He felt defensive and didn't like it.

"Because you scared me too, moron."

He didn't like being called a moron, but he'd refrain from judgement until she explained.

"You're good looking, a pro athlete, and larger than life in our town. All the woman were gaga over you, and you lorded it over everyone."

"I did not."

She shrugged. "I thought you did. It didn't help that I found you pretty sexy."

"Oh, well. That's okay then." He smiled.

"It's not," she snapped, "because after you seemed to be so different than the rest of the man-children in this town, you ended up being worse than all of them."

His smile faded. "Nora?"

"I'm sorry. I guess I'm still mad about you ghosting me. Deacon, that hurt. I thought we were friends. We had a great time out. I really liked you, and you burned me.'

"I know." He groaned. "I suck. I told you that."

"Yes, you did. But you can see why it's hard to open up again. I mean, you told a very similar story, having trust issues, with the ex who will not be named."

"I like that. Not be named. She's not important anymore." He nodded.

"But she *is* still important, or you wouldn't have been so dismissive with me." Nora watched him.

The conversation seemed to be heading in a bad direction. Deacon knew the signs.

"You're right." His agreement seemed to nonplus her, because she blinked up at him, startled. "I'm still carrying around the scars carved into me by someone I'd loved. I'm sorry you had to bear the brunt of her actions."

"Oh, well." Nora blushed. "I understand."

"Do you?" Time for her life story. "Your turn. Why are you so..." *Careful, Deacon.* "Wary around men? Or is it just me?"

She groaned. "I have to confess my dirty secrets since you did the same."

"Yep."

"Well, it's not that big a deal. My life isn't nearly as dramatic as yours has been." She sighed. "It's kind of boring, to be honest. I grew up here. I have great parents, and I dated my share of boys. Then I went to college and dated my share of men. No one seemed to stick. It's like I'd find guys I liked. We had things in common, then things would eventually fizzle out."

He let her talk, feeling the frustration she didn't quite name.

"Becca got married and had a baby. She found love with an amazing man." Nora turned toward him with a sweet smile. "Neal was a great guy. He loved Becca so much; you could see it when they were together. My parents have that. And it's what I've always wanted. Yeah, I love my career, and I'm a different person than the naïve young girl who wanted to get married and have babies. But deep down, I still want to find someone special."

He had the feeling she was a lot more like that naïve young girl than she wanted to admit.

"Neal died, and Becca lost it. It was so sad. Neal was like a brother, and we all grieved his loss. But again, it was Becca's husband. Becca's family. Becca's son who needed his aunt. I guess I felt like I never measured up to my larger-than-life cousin. She's amazing and beautiful."

"So are you."

Nora shook her head. "I'm not saying that so you'll compliment me."

"I'm not saying anything but the truth. Yeah, Becca's great. You're prettier than she is."

Nora blinked. "Oh." She blushed and glanced back at the lake. "Anyway, life just kept moving. I dated here and there, but this is a small town. A while ago, I spent some time away in Portland on a special project and met a guy."

Her voice had deepened, and he knew this particular guy had meant something to her.

"Flynn and I fell hard for each other in less than a week. I never told anyone this, and you have to swear you won't ever tell."

He crossed his heart. "Nora, I told you things I've never told anyone. Not even Roy."

She studied him and nodded. "Okay, well, Flynn and I were engaged."

A hollow feeling settled in his belly. "Oh?"

"For all of three weeks. I was so excited. I felt like I'd finally found my soulmate."

"When was this?"

"About two years ago." Nora looked at him once more, her smile sad. "But the engagement was a mistake. We both knew it, but we wanted the same thing. We were tired of dating and wanted to find someone and settle down."

"How did you know it was a mistake?"

"We actually talked about what we wanted to do after the wedding. And things started to fall apart right there. I wanted a small wedding with my family and friends. He wanted a big destination wedding. Then he wanted to travel the world and live in a van while we wrote a travel blog." She crossed her eyes, making him laugh. "I don't mind travel, but I'm not living in a van for twelve months. Nope."

"What did you want?"

"It's stupid."

"Tell me." Intrigued, he waited.

She watched him, as if gauging for a reaction. "I wanted to get married and have kids. We'd live here in Hope's Turn, where I'd continued to write my book and work on editorial pieces. And he'd work in town doing freelance writing. We could make it work. I know we could have." She shrugged. "But he didn't want to have children right away. I'd just hit thirty-three, and my biological clock was ticking so hard it was about to explode." She grinned. "I think that might have scared him."

It doesn't scare me. The thought took him aback. Was he really that ready for children and a family? To settle down with one woman who could so easily turn the tables and screw him over whenever she felt like it? His heart hammered, and he wondered why he continued to worry about a future that might never happen.

"You okay? It's no big deal, Deacon. I'm over it all."

"Are you?" He stopped her when she would have protested. "Because I'm realizing that Rhonda left her mark. And I'm thinking this Flynn guy left one too."

"He wasn't that important, to be honest." She looked thoughtful. "But maybe what he represented is what still hurts. I wanted to marry him so bad…but I never told my mom or dad about him. Becca had no idea I was dating him either. It was like he was my little secret, my own man, my own love."

"Was it love? Do you still miss him?"

She watched him, frowning. "No. I don't. I was infatuated, I think. And Flynn was great, but the idea of what he could be to me was even greater." She blinked. "Wow. Look at us having deep discussions together. It wasn't too long ago we were fighting all the time."

"In my defense, it wasn't fighting so much as protecting myself from verbal darts. So more like surviving."

"See, I did scare you."

"You still do." *Because I'm falling for you. Hard.* He cleared his throat, wishing her smug satisfaction didn't make him like her so much. "Because you have the worst taste in food."

"I—what? My food is yummy."

"Your food is toxic," he said drily. "Six boxes of toaster pastries? Doughnuts? Frozen dinners?"

"Hey, I didn't want to cook. And no one said you had to eat it." She poked him in the chest. "Besides, you can't cook worth a damn. How great was my breakfast this morning?"

He had to admit, "Pretty damn good."

"Ha. Exactly." She tucked her arm in his and led him off the dock and back around the lake. "I'm glad we could talk about stuff. It's been weighing on me that no one might ever know I actually got engaged."

He felt protective, wanting to shield her from the hurt he could still feel in her. "Do your parents pressure you for grandkids? Mine used to. Then they saw how awful Rhonda was and how badly I took our divorce. Unfortunately, with Mitch and Becca now all happy and having babies, my mom is bugging me again."

Nora nodded. "My mom used to nag me about having children, but she stopped when I told her how hard it was to hear her and deal with the useless men in town."

"I'm sensing some man-hating there."

She squeezed his arm, and his heart raced from just being near her.

"Sorry. That sounds mean."

"It is mean."

She laughed. "I know. But I got bitter fast, and that bitterness might have lingered." She looked up at him, and when he said nothing to that, she smiled. "You don't look that bright, but you're smart not to comment."

"Thanks."

She chuckled. "I'm kidding. I'm tired of not finding the right guy." She sobered quickly enough. "Deacon…"

"What?" He pulled her to a stop so he could study her. "You okay?"

She tugged him to walk again, so he did. "I'm thinking of leaving town."

That stopped him in his tracks, which stopped her again. "*What?*"

"It's just… I guess part of me still *is* that naïve girl wanting a family. I don't think I can find it here."

"Do your parents know? Does Becca?" Panic had him tensing, so he deliberately relaxed his body.

"No one knows." She didn't look at him, staring at the lake. "Don't tell, okay? I'm still thinking it over. I just… Hope's Turn is a great place for families. For raising kids. For small town life."

"It's not that small. I think there are like 30,000 people here."

"That's not the point. I'm frustrated, and I'm getting way too angry and mean for a woman my age. Deacon, I'm almost thirty-five. If I wait too long, I won't be able to have kids anymore."

"What? Women are staring families in their forties now."

"But the risk of not having a healthy baby goes up the older you get."

"I guess." He let her lead them into their walk again, then turned them around, wanting to talk her out of her decision to leave back in the warmth of the cabin. "But—"

"Just forget I said anything. Okay?"

"But Nora—"

"Please?"

"Fine." He blew out a breath. "But you have to be super nice and super naked later."

She patted his arm. "I can handle the super naked. Super nice? That's pushing it."

135

❄

Two hours later, after a rousing game where Deacon owned all the good properties with hotels and she had to resort to bribery and the promise of sexual favors to get out of paying rent, Nora stood naked under her robe and fixed them some hot chocolate. She brought the mugs back to the bedroom, where Deacon had headed to change into his "after hot tub" clothes. Simon had at least packed Deacon reasonable clothing. Jenna would need a good talking to. Nora was super tired of wearing thongs, though Deacon seemed to love them.

She caught him in just a pair of sweatpants, no shirt, and marveled at the sheer breadth of the man. He didn't look like a guy years past his pro-athlete prime. Deacon had nothing but muscle, no fat that she could see. She'd always been a sucker for a nice body, and she'd never seen one nicer than Deacon's.

"You need a few tattoos," she told him, aware her voice sounded deeper than normal.

"Oh? Maybe your name over my shoulder?" He flexed and grinned. "Or your face? I could move my arm so that you're frowning or smiling, depending on the amount of tension in my deltoids."

"Ha ha." She smirked. "I definitely think you should avoid names on your body."

He nodded. "It's the kiss of death for any relationship. A few friends of mine got tattoos and divorces followed."

She agreed. "I dated a guy with his ex's name on his chest. It's hard to think about a future with a guy who has *Barb-and-Tom-4-Ever* stamped on his body."

"Yeah, because Barb is nowhere near as sexy as Nora." Deacon took the mug she handed him and sipped. "Oh, this is good." He watched her while he drank, and her body tingled all over, turned on from a little eye-fucking, as Deacon liked to call it. "Nora?"

"Yeah?"

"I want you to promise me something." He put his mug down, then took hers and placed it next to his.

"What?"

"What are you wearing under that robe?"

"Huh? Nothing. What did you want me to promise?"

"Nothing, hmm?"

"Deacon?"

He had her in his arms and breathless from his kiss in seconds. Then he spun her to face the wall and peeled the robe from her body.

"Deacon?"

"I'm right here. And right where I want to be."

CHAPTER 14

*D*eacon couldn't think past the need to have her. Skin to skin, in his arms, under his control. He couldn't stop thinking about what she'd said earlier, about leaving town.

Leaving him.

Deacon had put down ties in Hope's Turn. He had a brewery. Friends. Family. Hell, he had a niece to spoil and a nephew to coach. But without Nora, he feared nothing much would matter.

How the hell had the snarky beauty gotten under his skin so fast?

But those questions could wait. He had pretty Nora naked and caged between him and the wall, bent over just right…

He lowered his sweatpants to free the thick erection needing attention.

"Deacon?" she asked, breathy. "What are you doing?"

"Whatever I want," he said, knowing how much she loved when he took control.

He slid a hand around her front and cupped her breasts, pressing his cock against her lower back.

"Oh," she moaned.

He kissed her neck, sucking on the tender flesh of her throat. Then he kissed his way to her ear and whispered, "Promise me you won't leave before you talk to me."

"Wh-what?"

He nudged her ankles wider and pulled her hips back, then positioned himself between her legs, seeking the hot, wet warmth of her sex. "Promise me, Nora."

"Deacon."

He shoved hard inside her, and she gasped as he pumped, a driving need to dominate her into saying yes all he could think about. He sawed in and out, loving her moans, her breathy pleas for more. And the knowledge that nothing separated them, that he might just give Nora that baby she'd been wanting, spurred him to new heights of arousal.

"I'm gonna come inside you, so hard."

"*Yes,*" she moaned. "Yes, Deacon."

"Touch yourself. Come with me."

He watched her hand move between her legs, and the carnal need to consume her overwhelmed him. He gripped her hips and rode her into an orgasm that obliterated all thought, dimly aware of Nora coming as well.

He held himself there, connecting them, having poured everything he had into her.

What felt like an eternity later, Nora shifted, and he withdrew. But he didn't let her leave him. He turned her around and kissed her, cementing what he felt even if he couldn't say it yet.

"God, Deacon." She kissed him back and wound her arms around his neck, leaving her on tiptoe. "You feel so good inside me."

"Yeah, I do." He smiled. "Come on. Let's clean you up." He carried her into the bathroom, which caused her to shriek in surprise.

"Way to go all caveman on me."

"You mean *in* you."

"Very funny." She let him clean her up, watching him with that look he'd come to recognize as affection mixed with confusion. "We've been having a lot of sex without condoms."

"Yep."

"And I'm safe. But probably after Sunday we should use them."

"Whatever you want." *Yes.* She wanted more of him after this week.

She frowned. "We haven't been smart, you know. What if my body went weird, and I was suddenly pregnant?"

"What if you were?" He looked at her abdomen, wondering how it would feel to cup her swollen belly and know his baby sat there. Warmth and *love* filled him, and he knew he'd welcome a child with Nora. Knew she'd be an amazing mother.

An amazing wife.

He blinked. "Would you keep the baby?"

"What? Of course," she automatically replied, then tried to backtrack. "Well, it's a hypothetical situation. I mean, if you're asking about abortion and a woman's right to choose and—"

"No. I just meant, would you keep a baby you and I made together?" He stroked her taut stomach, awash in emotion and a longing he hadn't expected would feel so real.

"Oh, ah. Yes. I would."

He couldn't read the look she gave him, but she placed her hand over his on her stomach and smiled. "But that's not anything we need to think about right now."

He stared at their hands. "I could use a condom next time if you want."

"No, not while we're here. It feels better without them." She paused. "Unless you'd feel more comfortable wearing one?"

"Hell, no. I love leaving you all messed and sweaty."

"Now that's an image."

"Yeah."

She gently pushed his hand from her belly, and he watched it fall with regret.

Nora flushed and twirled her hair, a nervous tell, watching him with equal parts fascination and fear. The fear bothered him. "Deacon, this, you and me, is just sex. Nothing else. I mean, we're just casual. Right?"

"Just casual," he agreed—verbally. Mentally, he knew as well as she did they were much, much more.

She relaxed. "Right. No expectations."

And no fear of getting hurt without them.

Deacon understood. Hell, he sympathized. Yet he also heard all that Nora had said and didn't say. She worried about getting pregnant but didn't want to use a condom. Did she secretly want his baby? And why didn't that bother him the way it should? Because she'd insisted they remain friends with benefits that would only last the week, yet she'd already mentioned they would need condoms when they met again after Sunday.

The little liar wanted him. She *liked* him. A lot. Now he just had to get her to feel his level of affection, which felt a lot like love and scared the crap out of him.

Nora Nielson, terror of the town, had his heart in a vise and no idea that she could crush him with little effort. Just freakin' great.

He sighed.

"Deacon? Are we still doing the hot tub or what?" She scooted out from under him and put her robe back on.

"I am. I don't know about you, but I'm sore from all that work I did to get you off."

"Get me off?" She huffed. "Please. I gave myself an orgasm. You were just along for the ride."

"And it was a hell of a ride, wasn't it?" He grinned.

She grinned back. "Brag much?"

"You want me to do better? Because I'm pretty sure I can."

"Okay. I sense a bet coming."

"It will involve swallowing, so you know."

She rolled her eyes. "What is with guys and blowjobs?"

"So you don't care if I go down on you again?"

They headed out toward the hot tub.

"I'm not saying that," Nora protested. "Women need oral sex. It's like Vitamin D, only we need more than the sun to get our share."

"Vitamin O." Deacon snickered. "Yeah, right."

"Whatever. Get in the tub and prepare to lose."

Just being with Nora made him a winner, but Deacon knew better than to admit that and let the sexy Amazon get an even larger head. Bad enough she owned him and didn't know it.

So he joined her and proceeded to lose. And lose again, just to see her smile and know he'd put it there.

NORA LAY IN BED NEXT TO DEACON IN THE DARK AND WONDERED IF she'd lost her mind. Talk about babies and not using condoms had given her too many daydreams about marriage and babies she didn't and probably would never have. Not with Deacon.

Not that long ago the man had been dating someone else, acting as if Nora didn't exist. This secluded stay in the mountains had turned her into an idiot. What woman had unprotected sex continually, even while wondering "what if" about pregnancy?

She trusted Deacon not to give her any diseases, but he couldn't help giving her a baby.

God, I can't stop thinking about it! They had so much sex. It was as if fate had made up for all the bad choices Nora had made in the past, giving her a perfect week with a perfect man. Reality would never be so great, so she should just accept it and enjoy.

Except she kept seeing Deacon's hand on her belly, the wonder in his eyes, his smile.

She groaned quietly and turned over and found herself plastered against Deacon's chest.

He murmured in his sleep and hugged her closer, setting her on fire with that hot body. The man generated more heat than a roaring fire. And the sheets weren't helping. But when she shoved them off, her butt got cold, so she tugged them back, content to roast over Deacon's naked body.

He murmured her name and sighed, and she admitted to herself she'd started to fall in love with the man. It helped that he had his own issues, not a perfect mate at all.

He experienced jealousy. He held grudges. He didn't have all the answers or any idea how to have a meaningful relationship.

In fact, in a lot of ways he was just like Nora.

He might not be perfect, but could he be perfect for her?

She felt silly for even considering that. And even more stupid for having confided so much to Deacon. A deep trust had grown between them. But how had it formed? From the mind-blowing sex? Or from a deeper understanding of the man she now slept with?

Nora wished she could turn off her brain. Unfortunately, she'd woken to use the bathroom and had been unable to sleep for the past hour. Being near Deacon muddled her thinking, obviously. Her perceptions of him didn't jive with what she now knew. Deacon looked tough but underneath was sincere and kind. Despite the sarcasm he wielded like an extension of his armor, he was more vulnerable than she would have guessed.

Remembering all he'd said about his ex-wife, she felt compassion for a man who'd only wanted what Nora did—a family, someone to love.

She sighed.

"If you aren't going to sleep," Deacon murmured, "how about putting that mouth to better use?" He dragged her to meet his mouth for a kiss.

She sighed again, this time into warm lips. The kiss turned from gentle and teasing to hot in seconds. Nora sat up over him while Deacon played with her breasts. His hands moved over her body, lingering on her belly, which rekindled feelings of belonging and need. Then he shifted his fingers between her legs, grazing the slick nub that gave her such pleasure.

She moaned and ground over him, moving on his hand while he continued to tease her.

"You're so fuckin' hot, Nora," Deacon said. "Come on, baby, sit on my face."

She scooted up his body and did as he asked, taken by his skilled lips and tongue.

She was coming before she knew it, following his lead as he shifted her back down his body, over his cock.

"Ride me," he ordered, his voice like gravel.

Taking him inside her, she felt the whole of him so deep. "Fill me," she whispered, staring down at the shadow of him as she moved up and down, faster then slower, drawing out his pleasure in the hope of giving back what he'd so selflessly shared.

"God, Nora. Baby, you feel so good."

She couldn't see much in the dark, but that lack of vision enhanced her other senses. The tantalizing smell of Deacon's aftershave and sex, the feel of his coarse hair against her body, of the steely muscle under her. And the sounds of his lovemaking, his grunts and groans, showing her how much he loved her body.

"I love coming in you," he said.

"Me too." She imagined so much more, but she couldn't say it. Even admitting it to herself turned off the good inside her, bringing out angry worry and fears she couldn't shake.

But sex was real. As was the growing climax building inside her again.

He struck her so deeply inside, hitting that special spot that triggered moans and cries for more.

"Yeah. Oh fuck. I'm coming." Deacon shoved hard one final time and jetted inside her, his entire body tense.

She moved over him and touched off the sparks that blazed into another orgasm, the sensation overpowering.

And she continued to move, giving as much as taking, sharing with Deacon in the only way she knew how, the only way that felt safe.

Once she'd come back to herself, she lay flat over his chest, still joined, and felt him stroking her back.

"I love when you don't sleep."

She smiled. "It's not so bad when I have such a warm pillow."

"I run hot in bed."

"You sure do."

He chuckled. "I feel so good with you, Nora. You make me laugh."

"Laughter is good."

"So are orgasms. And your pussy."

She blushed, glad he couldn't see because he'd tease her for it. "Flatterer."

"Hey, I like the way you taste."

"Would you stop?"

He laughed. "I know you're blushing. After just fucking me dry, you're embarrassed. Man, you're cute."

"It's dark. How can you tell?"

"I just can. I have superpowers."

"A super cock, maybe."

"It is pretty awesome. Want to hold it?"

She giggled, feeling as immature as a teenager and having fun. "I am holding it." She clamped down on him inside her. "Feel?"

"Fuck. That's so good." He groaned. "Is it bad that I want to keep loving you until I just can't get it up anymore?"

Loving you could mean many things to many people. To Nora, it had always meant the emotion. Affection, care.

"The day you can't get it up is the day we're done," she teased, telling herself to mean it. After all, she and Deacon were just casual. Just in it for the sex. Right?

He snorted. "As if that will ever happen. Guess that means you're stuck with me." After a moment, he wrapped an arm around her back, hugging her. "Relax, my tiny Amazon. I know. I know. You just want me for my body. I'm to be used and abused."

"Abused?"

"You just mauled me with your vagina. I'm your helpless slave." As if to emphasize that fact, he arched up into her, nudging inside her.

Where they remained connected, physically. And emotionally—at least, for Nora.

"Just remember that."

Yeah, Nora, remember it's only about sex.

He chuckled. "Sure thing, baby."

She had the sense he was just humoring her. But as the pleasure settled into her bones, she found her peace and relaxed into his arms, finally able to sleep.

CHAPTER 15

*M*onday afternoon, Nora sat in Becca's house and stared without seeing at her niece in Becca's arms.

"Hello? Earth to Nora. Are you going to wrap that present, or do you want to hold Ava so I can?" Becca asked.

"Huh? Oh sure. I'll hold her."

"That's the easy job," Becca complained, though she wore a smile, glowing with contentment.

"Where's Mitch?"

"Helping Roy at River Rip Brewing. When Deacon was out due to the snow, Mitch offered to help Roy out until you guys got back." Becca shot Nora knowing look and handed off her baby.

"What?"

Becca raised a brow. "You blush anytime I mention his name."

"Who? Mitch?"

"Oh please. Deacon Flashman. Ha! See? Right there. Your face is red."

"Shut up."

"So what happened up at the cabin? I swear, Mitch won't tell me anything."

"Nothing to tell."

"Liar. I know what happened."

"What?" Nora looked down at Ava, who looked around her with wide eyes and didn't make a fuss. So beautiful. Nora thought again to Deacon's hand over hers on her own belly.

Nope. Not gonna happen. When I have kids, I'm going to have the husband first. That's the plan.

Yet the plan was sucking, because she had no husband or baby. And probably never would while stuck in Hope's Turn.

"You and Deacon had sex," Becca announced at the exact same instant Mitch, Deacon, and the dog entered the living room.

Mitch stared, wide-eyed, between Nora and Deacon. "What?"

"You told her?" Deacon asked with a frown.

Nora glared at the big mouth. "No, I did *not* tell her anything. But you just did."

He blinked. "Oh. Sorry." Then the lug smiled. "But it was good, right?"

"I swear to you, right now, Deacon Flashman. If you high-five your brother, I will kick you in the nuts. Hard."

Mitch subtly lowered his hand.

"As if I'd do that." Deacon huffed. "I'm thirty-nine years old, Nora."

She saw him hold his hand behind his back and heard a slap. "I saw that!"

"It was a low five. You said no high five."

Becca shook her head at her husband, who approached Nora to take his daughter into his arms. "Honestly, Mitch. Grow up."

"Hey, you're the one talking about her sex life." He cuddled his daughter. "I was with this guy all day, and he said nothing."

To which Deacon shot Nora an accusing look.

To her chagrin, she knew she had only herself to blame for letting Becca badger her about the cabin.

Nora and Deacon had left yesterday, driving home and parting as friends. They'd agreed to remain private about their time together, knowing their family would prod and make their own assumptions. Which Becca had.

"What Nora and I do is no one's business," Deacon said firmly, shocking Nora that he'd put a stop to any questions before she could. "We're friends. That's all you need to know." He watched his brother. "Kid or no kid, I will put a hurt on you if you say whatever's on that tiny brain of yours."

Mitch opened and closed his mouth. "Right. So, ah, do you want lunch?"

Becca frowned. "What are you doing home? I didn't hear you come in."

Mitch shrugged. "We got finished earlier than we'd thought, so we headed back here. Deacon wants to swim. I thought you'd be at Nora's."

"I was going to, but I figured this would be a perfect time to wrap Simon's presents while he's not here."

Deacon crouched down to get a look, and his proximity made Nora's mouth water. He smelled like a subtle blend of pine and spice. She wanted to lick him up. In jeans and a Seahawks sweatshirt, he looked handsome as sin.

Fortunately, he kept his attention on the video games Becca was wrapping. "Oh yeah. Those are all the kids were talking about during the season."

"Please. You know you want them too," Mitch said.

"Well, yeah. How can I trounce Simon if I don't have the latest games?" Deacon grinned.

Nora's heart continued to run laps in her chest.

"What about you, Nora? What do you want for Christmas?" he asked as he turned to watch her.

They faced each other, only a few inches of space between them.

The charged silence evaporated when Mitch cleared his throat.

"Oh, ah, turkey sandwich for me, Bro," Deacon said, still watching Nora.

"Not what I asked, but Becca and I will go make some."

"We will?" Becca asked. "Okay. Join us in the kitchen when you're done staring at each other." She snickered and left with Mitch.

The open floor plan gave the couple a clear view of Deacon and Nora, but Nora didn't care. She hadn't seen Deacon in a whole day, and now she felt normal, being near him again.

"Hi." He smiled.

She smiled back. "Hi."

He glanced over his shoulder then stole a quick kiss. "Been wanting to do that since forever," he whispered. "Sorry the cat's out of the bag about us."

"That was my fault." *Us? What us is there?*

"So, um, I know you wanted to go back to normal. But I'm lonely at home." He made a sad face.

"Yeah, right." A pang of jealousy struck. "I'm sure you're busy fielding calls from lonely, single women."

"Nope. Just waiting for one smart-mouthed brunette to call." He sighed. "She still hasn't."

Nora couldn't hide her grin. "You miss me?"

"Like crazy." He stood and pulled her up with him. "Come over tonight?"

"For what? A booty call?"

"Nope. For dinner."

She frowned and kept her voice low. "No sex?"

"Why? You desperate for me already?" he teased.

Yes. "No. But dinner isn't sex."

"No, it's two people eating food together," he said slowly, but she saw the twinkle in his eyes. "Are you afraid of me, Nora?"

"Please." She huffed. "I'm afraid of no one but Simon when he's visiting and there's no food in my house."

"We're all afraid of that," he agreed. "Teenagers need food. He's a right little bastard when he's hungry."

She laughed, because Simon could get pretty cranky. "Dinner, huh?"

"I'm buying."

The smart move would be to nix this idea of hanging out. They would meet for sex and only sex and keep it simple. So Nora said, "Well, okay. Because if you were going to cook, I'd have to say no." *Why do I never do the easy thing?*

"That's so mean." He smiled. "I love that about you."

She hated that her heart raced like crazy when he used the L word.

"Quit flattering me and let's get sandwiches. And if your brother keeps giving me that look, I'm telling your mom on him."

"Good call. Brenda Flashman is savage when her favorite is getting bullied."

Mitch heard him and frowned. "I'm Mom's favorite."

Deacon snorted. "You keep thinking that."

While they argued, Becca pulled Nora aside and said, "You and I are going to talk later, missy. Bet on it. Or else." She dragged a finger across her throat.

Nora sighed. At least she'd have a decent dinner to make up for what was sure to be an uncomfortable interrogation later.

"Here, hold Ava," Mitch said to Deacon. "Becca, come help me make lunch."

"Okay, but we can't take too long. Simon will be home soon, and we have to wrap and hide the presents."

Mitch smiled. "No problem. I got you covered, babe."

While the married pair flirted, Nora watched Deacon handling Ava and blurted, "You're going to make a good father someday."

Fortunately, her cousin and Mitch didn't hear her.

Deacon's eyes widened, then a blush covered his cheek. He gave her a shy smile. "I think that's the nicest thing you've ever said to me, Nora."

"Don't let it go to your head," she grumbled and stroked Ava's fine hair. "She's so pretty."

"Someday you'll have one just like her." Deacon held Ava's tiny fist wrapped around his finger. "Baby Nora. I bet she'll be adorable, just like her mom." He looked into her eyes, and she quickly backed away, confused at what she saw.

And what she felt.

Love.

DEACON SIGHED AND DOWNED HIS BEER. WEDNESDAY EVENING, HE stood with Roy at the bar, overseeing the staff and the crowded pub. "She's avoiding me, Roy."

Roy groaned. "Are we talking about Nora *again?*"

"I was holding Ava and looking into her beautiful eyes."

"Ava's?"

"No, Nora's. They're brown, so pretty. Dark and deadly, that's Nora." He sighed. "Man, she's amazing."

"So, how did you manage to blow it this time?"

Deacon shrugged. "No idea. Maybe she saw that I'm falling for her."

"Fallen, you mean."

"What?"

"Nothing." Roy coughed. "So, she's nervous because you're coming on strong?"

"She's trying to keep our relationship all about sex. But I want more. I invited her to dinner. She said yes then called later to cancel. I haven't seen her in two days."

"Do you think she's just not into you?"

"No. I *know* she likes me. Maybe even more than just 'likes.' But she's scared."

"I'm scared of you." Roy met Deacon's gaze. "You have a resting bitch face."

"That's a girl thing."

"Yep, like I said."

"Ass." But Deacon laughed. "Nora has mean down to a science. Roy, man, I think I love her."

"Shit. That deserves a second round." Roy got them two bottles of the special IPA and toasted him. "To you and Nora, may you one day not scare off the love of your life."

"That's a little much."

"Nope. It's not. Nora's great. Jess and I like her. She doesn't take your shit, and you've never been happier than when you're with her or talking about her. She won't see you? Go make a move. Call her on her bullshit."

"She'll dump me."

"So she'll dump you. Make her see how miserable she'll be without you."

"How do I do that?"

"Hey, do you see a crystal ball anywhere? No? Me neither. I'm just the idea man. Make it happen on your own dime."

"Some friend you are."

"Hey, I covered for you while you played in the snow for a week."

"Technically I played in the hot tub."

Roy glared "Yeah, that detail makes it so much better."

Deacon chuckled. "Seriously, thanks for covering for me."

"You did your share with the invoices online. And thank Mitch. He helped a ton. But even without him, we would have been okay. I got you, man."

"I know. You're always there for me."

MARIE HARTE

"Remember that this Christmas. Jess wants to take extra time to go down and see the family in Texas."

"You got it. I owe you."

"Nah. We're even. Now go figure out how to win back Nora while I deal with Ericka." He made a face. "She's the worst bartender we've ever had."

"I know. Which is why I told you not to hire her. But you fell for her sterling resume. All her T's and A's crossed." T's and A's—or more to Roy's level, her tits and ass.

"Whoa, whoa, now. I'm a married man." Roy looked offended.

"Whatever. She batted her eyes and you, a sucker, told her with a little training she'd be just fine. You hired her, you fire her."

"I know, I know. And for the record, it wasn't her T's and A's," Roy muttered. "More like her soft voice, baby blue eyes, and her screwdriver. She really knows how to make a good one. But yes, I know, I'll take care of it." He paused. "Okay, maybe it was a little T, but not one word to Jess."

Deacon smirked. "I knew it. Hey, I noticed them too. But I didn't hire her."

"Go home." Roy stomped away to deal with Ericka, and Deacon texted Simon for a favor.

The smart-aleck had no problem giving him Nora's address—as well as notice of now two 'favors owed.' Deacon couldn't wait for the teen to call them in.

Amused despite himself, he drove to Nora's house, testing out one approach after another and deciding to wing it.

With any luck, he'd round to first, slide through second, and keep going for a home run.

And Mitch said he didn't know baseball.

156

CHAPTER 16

"Sorry, slick. I'd say you just struck out." Nora stood in the front doorway, eyeballing an incensed Deacon.

"You won't let me in? Come on, Nora. We know each other" He lowered his voice to add, "*Really* know each other."

"This is my home, and I'm sorry, but it's sacred." Yes, she was being childish, but she didn't think she'd sleep any better with memories of him in her place. She already couldn't sleep because she couldn't stop remembering him in the cabin—now forever associated with Deacon and a snowbound week of nonstop pleasure.

"Fine. Can we talk at my place then?" He continued to sound reasonable.

Which annoyed her. Shouldn't *he* be missing her to the point of wondering about his sanity? Shouldn't *he* be thinking hard over how bad it might *not* be to date? Nora missed him like crazy, and it had only been two days since they'd last been together. And no, it hadn't been all about missing sex, either.

She missed Deacon's smile, his sarcasm, his sense of humor. She missed touching him, seeing his joy in the little things. Watching him fall in love with his niece every time he held her…

"Why are you here?"

Deacon sighed. "Nora, the one thing I like best about you is that you don't bullshit. You're all about honesty."

"I am."

"Can't we be honest with each other…off the street?" he asked quietly.

He had her there.

"Yes, we can." She stepped aside. "Come in."

He entered her cute cottage and looked around, seeing the small space just as it was. Colorful but tiny, with a fluffy couch, a console table behind it, and coffee table in front of it, facing a wall with a small flatscreen TV. The adjoined kitchen was big enough to cook in but not large enough to host Deacon and Mitch side by side if she stood with them. Off the kitchen, there was just enough space for four chairs and a table.

Down the hall was a bathroom, and farther down her bedroom, which fit her queen size bed, a few bookcases, and a nightstand. And that was it. Home sweet home—all she could afford on her meager income in the small town which continued to see real estate values rise.

"You work in there?" he asked, pointing to the kitchen table, where her laptop sat.

"Yep. My office slash restaurant." She grinned and waved down at her clothes. "We're not fussy about who we feed there." Her overlarge sweatshirt hung off one shoulder, showing the strap of her fitted tank. She wore baggy shorts and long socks and looked like a runway tragedy.

But she had a warm apartment, so she didn't much care what she looked like, only that she was comfortable while staring at her laptop screen, suffering from writer's block and Deaconitis—a need for the big man standing before her.

His eyes warmed as he looked her over and his gaze caught on her hair pulled back into a ponytail high on her head. "You look like a college grad."

In a breathy voice she asked, "Oh, is it fantasy-time?"

"I wish." He sighed. "Okay, let's talk." He moved past her to the kitchen and sat down with a glance at her screen, his eyes narrowing.

Remembering she'd been researching about pregnancy and hormone levels for her book and not wanting him to get the wrong idea, she closed her laptop and blurted, "It's research for my book. Not about me."

"Um, okay."

She sank into a chair near him and waited.

He shook his head. "No, thanks. I'm good."

"What?"

"You were going to ask if I wanted something to drink, but I'm fine." He smiled through his teeth.

She snorted. "As if I have manners."

At that he grinned sincerely. "Nora, you are truly unique."

"Thanks?"

He laughed and leaned over to tug on her hair.

"Hey."

"It's not my fault. It was begging me to pull it."

"I bet you were a terror in elementary school."

Deacon grinned. "I really was." He said no more, watching her.

A full minute passed.

She swore. "Damn it. Fine. We're just supposed to have sex, but you're making this relationship way too complex."

"How?'

"Dinner? What's dinner? And don't you dare say it's a meal between hungry people!"

He sat back in his seat and clasped his hands over his middle. "I wanted to be with you."

"For what?" She hated feeling nervous. Right now Deacon resembled a rock; she could have passed for a feather in the wind, drifting this way and that.

"For companionship," he offered kindly. "Because you're real, and I know you're not out to use me for anything I don't want. You're a funny person, and we enjoy each other. Are those not great reasons to hang out?"

"Yes, they are." She felt miserable. "I'm sorry, but this is getting complicated."

"You're right."

"I am?" God, did he feel something more for her too?

"I want you. I want to come inside you, eat you up, fuck you standing, sideways, sitting. In the shower, the snow, the—"

Blushing, she held up a hand. "Okay, okay. I get it."

"But your body isn't all I like about you. You're the whole package. I made a mistake before, because I was scared. Our first date was better than any date I'd ever had. I loved it, so I left and tried to find interest in safe, boring people. That sounds mean, but they're all boring compared to you."

Pleasure unfurled. "You're just saying that."

"Um, yes, I am just saying that. Should I write it instead?" He cocked his head.

"Don't be an ass," she snapped. "You know what I mean."

"I truly don't." Deacon's eyes narrowed, his gaze roaming her face. "Am I not supposed to like you?"

"No. I'm incredible. You should love me." Realizing what she'd said, she blushed even harder. "I mean, I—"

"I know what you mean."

"Stop it."

"What?"

"Stop looking at me like...that." *Like you love me. Because it's freaking me out!*

"How am I looking at you?"

Panicked and not sure she wouldn't just blurt out how much she was coming to love him, she stood and whipped off her sweatshirt and tank.

As expected, he stared, wide-eyed, at her bare breasts.

"You're here. I want sex. You just admitted you want it too. So? Let's do it." She paused. "I don't have any condoms."

"I have one in my jacket," he murmured, still staring at her body.

So easy. She had to hide a smile. "Then how about I—"

"You want to distract me?" His gaze hardened and returned to her face. "How about you do what you need to, but I'm going to talk?"

"I...what?"

"I came over to talk. You want sex. Okay, I'm yours." He held his arms out. "You take what you need, but I'm getting this off my chest." Yet he couldn't stop staring at all of her.

Determined not to hear what she wasn't ready for, Nora took the fun, cowardly way out and stripped down to nothing. Then she took off Deacon's jacket and shirt while he rambled about feelings and truth and more feelings. Blah blah.

"Move your chair. Scoot this way." She motioned for him to move so she could kneel between his feet.

He moved his chair and did his best to focus on her face. "Nora, this is real, between us. I'm not fucking around. I like you. A lot. I…" He trailed off as she unzipped him and took him out, his erection evidence of how much he loved having her near. He was good and hard, his tip shiny with need.

Deacon cleared his throat and tried to make eye-contact, but she saw his gaze constantly dipping to her breasts. "I have feelings for you, Nora. We're good together." He sounded ragged.

She blew a breath over his cock, and he shuddered.

No longer afraid but high on her own power, she bent her head to her task.

"I know we can be good together. I…" He closed his eyes, tilted his head back, and groaned while he palmed the back of her head. "*Fuck.* Nora, you are *killing* me."

She bobbed faster, taken with his moans, the stiffness of his shaft, how taut his thighs had grown.

"Nora, baby. Come on. Sit on me."

She sucked harder.

"I'm gonna come. You'll have too much to swallow," he tried to joke but pumped up into her mouth. "Please. Sit on me. Up and down. Let me come inside you."

She wanted that. A little too much. But the threat of pregnancy loomed too large to ignore. So, she bore down and swallowed when he cried her name.

When he finished, she pulled away and licked her lips. "Yum."

Deacon didn't bother tucking himself back in. He exploded out of his chair and hauled her into his arms. Then he hurried down to her bedroom, threw her on the bed, and gave her the best oral sex of her life.

When finished, he stood, tucked his once-again erect cock back into his jeans, and zipped up. He stared down at her, looking satisfied and not as off-balance as she might have hoped. "That was amazing. I know you're busy, so I'll leave. Call me when you're ready to talk." He waved goodbye and walked away. "Thanks for the sex," he called over his shoulder.

After a pause, in which he'd likely grabbed his shirt and jacket, the front door slammed closed. But she couldn't move, too sated to think clearly.

Not much later, Nora realized she'd come across as a sex-starved fool while Deacon had been making a point about being honest. She owed it to him to be the same—to a point. She had her well-being to protect after all.

She wouldn't go after him now. She'd give it a day or two then talk to him. When she'd gotten herself together enough to speak to the man without remembering how turned on she'd been while blowing him.

A girl had to have some dignity, after all.

Friday night, River Rip Brewing had a full parking lot and a hopping band thrumming some catchy alt-rock for the crowded pub. People drank, ate, danced, and shouted to be heard over the music. It was a place Nora would have loved to frequent with a date or group of friends…if she'd had either.

She looked around for someone in charge and saw Roy tending bar. He saw her and waved her over. "Hi, Nora. Welcome to the best place in town. Want a beer? On the house!"

"Why are you behind the bar?" Wasn't he an owner?

"I used to bartend back in my days after college. It's fun when you don't have to do it all the time. Actually, I'm filling in for one of our guys who called in sick. So can I get you that beer? Our seasonal brew is amazing."

"Thanks, but no. I'm here to see Deacon. Is he around?"

"Oh, go on upstairs. He's finishing up some paperwork but should be done soon. And I know he'd love to see you."

She wondered exactly how much Roy *did* know about Deacon and Nora. Probably as much as Becca, since the bossy woman had strong-armed Nora into confessing everything last night. Nora had been doing her best to avoid her cousin since Monday, but Simon had tricked her into coming by the tea shop to help earlier in the day—only for Nora to run into Becca there.

Simon hadn't even looked sorry for his traitorous actions.

So now, two days after jumping the man and just five days until Christmas, Nora had to talk to Deacon like a mature, adult woman. Not a ninny trying to divert her man's attentions with sex, though that had worked like a charm.

She smiled to herself as she moved into the back corridor and went up the stairs. She walked down a short but wide hallway and saw three doors. One led to a common restroom, the other was labeled storage, and the final one said *THE BOSSES* on it. Had to be Deacon.

She lifted her hand to knock and heard raised voices inside. So she did the responsible thing…and listened at the door.

"Damn it, Deacon. You have to come back to me. You told me you loved me," came the disturbing voice of a woman.

What the hell?

"Meghan, I think you have me confused with someone else."

"You said it!"

"No, I didn't. I have said *I love you* to a total of two women in my entire life. One is my mother. The other's my ex-wife, and that was a *very* long time ago. Now what exactly do you want? Because we are not a couple and never will be."

"You're an ass."

"A busy ass, so if you could say whatever you need to say and get out?"

Nora blinked, in shock. She'd never heard him use that cold tone before. He sounded curt, frustrated, and annoyed. But not like his usual annoyance with her, which often had a hint of amusement in it. Nora could tell he didn't like this woman.

"Fine. I didn't want to let you know like this, but I'm…"

"Meghan, just say it. Please."

"I'm pregnant."

The world stopped.

No. He. Did. Not. Nora couldn't believe it. She'd been prepared to give him a chance, to try to see where they might be together. But not if he had impregnated someone else!

To her surprise, Deacon laughed. "Oh, that's a good one. You know that's a lie. I always wore a condom with you. Hell, with every woman I've been with."

Not with me. Unless he's lying to her… Nora wanted badly to believe she was special. She trusted Deacon. Didn't she?

He continued, "You and I have been done for a while."

"There was a hole in one of them," Meghan said, her self-satisfaction obvious. "I know because I put it there."

Nora shoved open the door, needing to see the voice that went with the venom. "Oh my God. You poked holes in his condoms?"

"Nora?" Deacon sat up straight in his chair then quickly stood. "What are you doing here?"

"Two-timing me already?" Meghan, a flashy redhead with large breasts and a striking face, asked him.

Nora focused on the woman, irritated to find her so pretty. "You poked holes in his condoms to get pregnant?"

Meghan gave her a disdainful onceover. "Who the hell are you?"

Deacon scrubbed his face. "Nora, ignore her. She was just leaving." He called downstairs. "Roy, Meghan snuck in. Get the cops for me, would you? And send up Melia and Tanya to escort her downstairs. Thanks." He hung up.

Meghan stamped her foot. Nora didn't think women did that outside of movies and TV. "Damn it. I'm pregnant! By you!"

"By me?" Nora asked, just to annoy the witch.

"Shut up. By *him!*" Meghan pointed a perfectly manicured nail his way.

"This is what turns you on?" she asked him, ignoring the redhead to aggravate her even more.

"No. Which is why we broke up." Deacon shook his head. "I'm trying to be nice, Meghan. But I won't tolerate lies."

"My lawyer will be talking to you."

"Good," Nora cut in. "Then have him tell you the penalties for rape in this state. Because poking holes in a condom is a punishable offense by law."

Meghan didn't look so sure of herself. "It is?"

Nora nodded, not having a clue, but she swore she'd seen a Law & Order episode about that very thing at one time or another. And heck, if it wasn't illegal it certainly should be.

Deacon sighed. "It doesn't matter because—"

"I'm not pregnant, you ass." Meghan glowered at Deacon. "I thought maybe we could try again. But clearly I was forgetting why we broke up."

"Because I ended things?" Deacon said drily.

Meghan continued her rant. "You're pathetic. The only good thing you have going for you is that huge dick. Other than that you're a sad, washed-up loser."

Deacon's expression cleared, his eyes hard. Meghan was pushing buttons, Nora could tell. And she didn't like the idea he might be hurting because of this awful woman.

So she said, "I don't think you meant washed-up. He never *washed up*, technically. He could be a has-been though. Deacon, you okay with has-been?"

He met her gaze and visibly relaxed. "Yeah. I was great, so I 'had been' a superstar. It was an injury that did me in. Although, technically, I guess I could be washed-out."

"Maybe."

"Shut the fuck up," Meghan shouted. "I don't care who you are," she said to Nora. "But there's no way you could ever replace me."

"You got that right," Nora agreed. Who wanted to stand in for a shrewish user?

167

Deacon laughed. "Exactly."

Meghan looked confused.

Deacon turned to the woman and pointed at the door. "Meghan, for the last time, get out. I'm not your pretend-baby's daddy. I always provided the condoms we used, because I didn't trust you then. And I sure the hell don't trust you now. Get out before I sue you for libel and smear your name all over the paper."

"Sorry, Deacon. Technically that's slander," Nora had to correct him. "Libel is when it's written defamation."

"Shut. Up!" Meghan screeched at her before turning to Deacon. "As if anyone would believe you," she sneered.

Nora smiled. "Well, when I tell them how you tried to blackmail him… Oh wait. Deacon, blackmail is definitely illegal. You should make sure you tell the police that when they arrive. And I'll testify to everything that went down in here."

"Screw both of you." Meghan stormed away in a huff just as two women appeared to escort her away.

"Boss?" one of them asked at the doorway.

"Thanks, Tanya. Just make sure she leaves without destroying the bar, okay?" She and her friend gave him a thumbs up and left behind a complaining Meghan.

Deacon shut the door behind them and groaned. "What a day."

"Just…wow. That was one of your exes?"

He sat against his desk and watched her with broody eyes. "Yeah. See why I left?"

"You sure can pick 'em."

He cocked a brow while still looking at her.

Realizing what she'd intimated, she added, "Present company excluded, of course."

"Of course." After a pause, he asked, "Not that I'm not happy to see you, but why are you here?"

"Now *that* is the million dollar question."

CHAPTER 17

*D*eacon felt exhausted. Between feeling as if he'd screwed things up with Nora—who might actually *be* pregnant with his baby—dealing with some missed paperwork he hadn't anticipated in addition to all the year-end festivities, and then having Meghan show up, he needed a break from life.

Then to have Nora appear at the worst possible time…

She studied him, frowning.

"I wasn't kidding," he said, needing Nora to know. "I never fully trusted her and always supplied my own condoms." He answered her next question. "Yes, you and my ex-wife are the only women I've ever not worn protection with. My ex took birth control when we were supposed to be trying for a baby. So yeah, I'm not big on trust."

But I trusted you. And I thought you trusted me.

Women baffled him. Take Meghan after all this time… "Damn. Why would Meghan show up like that? I made it clear we were through weeks ago." He shook his head. "I mean, she only wanted me for my money. Nothing has changed since we broke up."

Nora didn't answer, but she did step closer. Then, without being prodded, she hugged him.

The act took him by surprise. As if sucker-punched, he folded in on her and just clung.

God, he'd missed her.

She stroked his head, tunneling her fingers through his hair, and just let him lean on her. Nora Nielson, a good hundred plus pounds lighter, smaller, yet so damn strong she could hold his sorry ass up.

Coming back to himself, he gave her a squeeze then gently nudged her back a step.

"Better?"

He nodded. "Yeah, thanks."

She cleared her throat. "I listened at the door when I heard her yelling at you. Man, what a bitch."

"Yep."

"You seriously traded up when you met me."

He smiled but felt his joy leech away when her mirth left her. "Deacon, I have a few things to say to you."

His nerves raced. It had taken him a while to put it together, but seeing what she'd been researching on her laptop, then the way she'd dealt with him, so sexually and brazenly the past Monday, he'd put two and two together. He must have gotten Nora pregnant during their week at the cabin. He'd googled it, and sometimes women could know as soon as four or five days after the fact. Some tests showed increased levels of hCG, which she'd been researching.

Any notion she might have intentionally gotten pregnant just didn't compute. Nora was Nora—honest, aggravating, and loving. She'd never trick a man into a baby. Rhonda, on the other hand, and even Meghan, he could see trying something so low.

He was overjoyed to know he might soon be a father. And scared. And excited. And afraid. But most of all, the notion of having created such joy with *Nora*, the only woman he wanted, put his life in perspective.

He trusted her wholeheartedly.

Because he loved her.

But she had to love him back. And she had to be honest about things with him. Knowing how much of a shock it must have been, he had decided to let her come to him about the pregnancy. But not today. Not when Meghan stood in front of him with her lies and accusations.

"Just so you know, I really want kids. Just not with Meghan," he said quickly.

She nodded. "Okay. I get that."

He waited.

"I'm sorry I jumped you the other night."

"Oh, well, no problem." She'd probably been worried and stressed about the baby, not ready to talk about it. And maybe her hormones had been driving her. He smiled. "You can jump me anytime."

"No." She took in a big breath and let it out loudly. "I'm sorry. I should have just talked to you like a normal person. Instead, I tried to distract you with sex."

"I know. I went along anyway."

"You're easy."

He grinned.

"But I wanted you to know that I… care about you."

"I care about you too."

She frowned. "I feel affection for you."

"I feel the same."

Her frown darkened. "I'm falling for you, dumbass. Would you just be quiet and let me say it?"

Hearing what he'd been hoping to hear for so long, he did his best to bite back his grin and waited, his heart full.

"I'm not good at relationships. I told you that. And you worry me."

"I'd never hurt you, Nora."

"You already did," she said bluntly. "I thought we were friends, and you ditched me. I know, you've apologized. Several times. But, see, it had taken everything in me to open up and date you that first time. It still stings. And now, we had that amazing time in the cabin that didn't feel real. You're so much funner—yes, that's a word, don't try me— sexier, and kinder than I thought you'd be. Kind is good, Deacon. Don't scowl."

"Can I talk now?"

"No. Not yet. I want you to know that I'm not easy. I want things. I want marriage and babies and forever. I want what my parents have." Her eyes teared, but he held back his instinctive need to offer comfort as she continued. "I want what Becca, Mitch, and Simon have. A family. But it takes time to build trust."

When he still said nothing, she admitted, "I want that with you."

She made no mention of the baby, but she'd said so much he'd been dying to hear. "Nora, no one knows what the future holds. Your parents and my parents got lucky. Mitch and Becca are new, and let's face it, they've had different lives than we have. But I haven't felt this way about a woman in forever." He closed the distance between them and cupped her cheeks in his hands. He wanted badly to confess how much he loved her, but a part of him needed to wait, to assess, to be surer. "I want to give you everything. We seem to want the same things. Family. To fall in love and stay in love. But we can't know the future."

"I know." She curled a strand of hair around her finger, saw him watching, and flushed. "You make me nervous. Off-kilter. I don't like that."

"I'm always hard around you," he confessed. "I have better control over my body. Usually. And you make me just as nervous. I'm always saying the wrong thing or making you upset with me. And I mean well."

She smiled. "You're kind of a big doofus."

"You're a small, mean-tempered doofus. But so sexy."

"So maybe we're made to be doofuses together."

"Can you make that word plural?" Deacon didn't think so.

"Is that a challenge for naked Scrabble, I hear?" She leaned up to accept his kiss.

"I think it is. But, well, maybe at my place this time? Since you let me see the wonder that is Nora's den, maybe you could come hang out at Casa Deacon?"

"I think maybe I could. Tonight?"

"Yeah." He kissed her, this time deepening their embrace. Though they'd been together two days ago, it felt like forever. He groaned. "If it wouldn't make working here awkward forever, I'd take you right now over my desk."

"Oh. I like that."

"But then I'll get hard every time I'm in here. And that could be weird with our employees."

She laughed. "I understand. Why don't I wait for you downstairs? The band is pretty good."

"I told you so."

"Maybe next time I'll bring a date," she teased.

He was serious when he said, "About that… If we're together, it's just us. I don't believe in cheating."

She gave him a wide, happy smile. "Good. Me neither."

"You've said you have issues. Well, I do too. Trust is huge with me."

"Yep, you have a mountain of issues."

He frowned at her tone. "You sound a little too chipper about that."

"I am. You're far from perfect. That makes you dateable."

"Because perfect is boring." He totally understood. Nora never bored him.

"Exactly." She kissed him once more, then reached between his legs and squeezed, bringing him close to orgasm.

"Fuck, Nora. Don't do that or I'll come in my pants."

She kissed him again and let go. "Mine." Then she took his hand and put it between her legs. "Yours. No one else's. That's about as basic as I can get."

He nodded, completely in love with this woman. "One question—how do you feel about hot wings?"

"Weird question, but I feel good about hot wings…unless you're trying to steal them off my plate. And anyone who eats celery should be shot."

"Right answer." *I am* so *going to marry this woman.* Yet he saw the hint of caution still in her expression and knew he had to tread carefully. Especially with a baby on the way. "I'll be down soon. We carry tons of sodas and juices too. Get whatever you want on me."

"You're damned right on you. And before you think I might be using you like the redhead with big boobs did, because we're dating, you're now entitled to free stuff at Bragg's Tea."

"I was before. Becca said. I'm family." Though he'd always made sure to pay.

"Bitch, please. I run that shop when she's gone, and I make the rules. You're in because of me."

"Yes, ma'am." He gave her a salute and laughed when she returned a one-fingered one of her own.

Then he got to work and left her to Roy and the band downstairs, anticipating the night to follow.

CHAPTER 18

They spent the next few days in glorious harmony. Deacon and Nora walked together, ate together, and spent their days making snarky comments over bad movies and even worse holiday shoppers. Nora had him help her fill in at the tea shop, and he used her to keep Roy in line when his friend decided to bring up the old days and Deacon's college years.

Deacon had never been so head-over-heels in love with anyone. Only one thing marred his happiness—she still hadn't confided in him about the baby.

They made love with condoms, which had confused him, but maybe she didn't want him to know. Or maybe she wasn't pregnant, and he'd misread her laptop. Yet every time he mentioned the word *baby*, she blushed. And she refused to drink alcohol or coffee lately, mentioning an odd bellyache when she did. Yet more evidence she had his bun in her oven. He wondered what she would think about a spring marriage, or if that might be pushing things.

Even his brother had mentioned how pleasant Deacon was to be around lately. Though Deacon and Nora kept things quiet around family, taking it slowly, they spent their waking moments together in private.

Like tonight, just three days from Christmas. And two from her birthday. They sat together for naked Scrabble, a new favorite game, in his den downstairs—what Nora had taken to calling his love nest. Between the large TV, pool table, and game table, they had a ton of fun. And that wasn't counting the fire pit outside, where just last night they'd roasted marshmallows.

The back bedroom had been prepped with lit candles, edible body butter, whatever that was, and some fuzzy handcuffs. Nora loved getting just a little kinky as much as he loved watching her while they made love. And it had been *making love* lately, much to his sexy girl-friend's chagrin.

He secretly laughed when she got that look, a baffled, thrilled, yet nervous expression, as if she didn't know what to do with his affection. Each had yet to confess their deeper feelings, but he felt it so much. And he knew she felt something close to it, at least. She watched him with gooey eyes when she didn't think he could see her. And she touched him a lot too, not sexually, but to keep that connection going.

Tonight, he'd set sodas on the table for them to drink while they tried to out-Scrabble each other. Nora was too good. While she wore a skimpy bra and her jeans and panties, he'd been reduced to boxers and socks.

"Xenophobe is spelled with an X, not a Z." He snorted. "Nice try."

"Oh, my bad." The titter in her false apology didn't fool him.

"Faker."

"You seem to be able to read me too easily." She frowned. "I'll have to come up with some new bluffs."

"Good luck with that. I've been reading Mitch since he was a toddler.

And I'm great at reading opposing team defense. I'm good at people." He paused. "Well, not women, obviously."

She frowned.

"What?"

She poked herself in the chest. "I'm a woman."

"Oh, right." He chuckled. "I was thinking you're more like a super woman and sexual dynamo all wrapped up in one person."

"That's nice." She smiled.

"I'm forgiven?"

"Maybe. If you let me use my Z."

"Dream on."

"Ass."

They continued to play, discussing the holiday and her parents.

"They're going on a cruise? That's awesome." Deacon liked Sue and Luke a lot. They reminded him of his own folks.

"They'd booked it a year ago. They almost canceled, but Becca told them to go. They can spend Christmas with Ava and Simon next year."

"My folks will be here. They had to go home after Ava was born, but they came back a week ago and have been staying with some friends outside town. Mitch said they arrived at his place two hours ago and expect me there for Christmas. I have my marching orders."

"Mitch said?"

He sighed. "I've been ducking my mom's calls." He paused. "I think Mitch might have mentioned something about you and me."

"Oh." She watched him. "What am I supposed to say now?"

"First, you take off that bra since you didn't use the Z."

"Hmm. I think not." She stood and stripped out of her jeans, giving him heart palpitations. Then she leaned over, giving him an up close and personal view of the lovely V between her full breasts as she stared at the tent in his shorts. "Good. My devious plan is working."

"What? To distract me with your body while we play? Not so much devious as obvious."

Her sly wink had him laughing.

"So, do you want me to confirm to your parents we're actually dating or what?"

He didn't want to push. "Only if you feel comfortable doing it." He wanted to shout to the world that she was his.

"You should tell them. You're the son."

"The son. I like that. With a capital T in *the*."

"You're an idiot. But apparently now you're my idiot."

He smiled.

"Your word next."

He made the word *extort,* using an X, with relish. "Triple word score. Eat it, Nielson."

"Bare it and I will," she said, snippy to the end.

"Lose the panties or the bra. Your choice."

The blasted woman took her top off.

"Just admit you lose," she said, her smile wide.

"I will if you let me come inside you. No condom."

She blinked. "Um, well, what if I get pregnant?"

Her way of asking how he felt about the baby? He smiled and patted his lap, and she left her chair to sit with him, her breasts brushed up against his chest and causing a deeper ache, this one between his legs. "Nora, if you were pregnant with my baby, I'd be the happiest man alive."

She gaped. "Seriously?"

Now she'll tell me. "Yeah. I'm ready for a family. But more, for children and a wife." He paused, seeing the shell shock in her face. "I'm not trying to rush you, but you did say you wanted kids. And there's no one I trust like I trust you. Or like." *Or love.*

"Oh, wow." Her eyes glistened with emotion. "Deacon, that means so much to me."

But she didn't tell him about the kid. Instead, she scooted off his lap to lose her panties while he quickly lost his socks and underwear.

Then she sat him back down and sank over him, already wet and ready. She rocked and kissed him, and he could do nothing but follow her lead, lost in her taste. Her touch.

He raised her up so he could suck her nipples, in lust with her body. But he needed to be inside her again, and she was too restless to let him play.

She slammed back over him and nearly caused his brain to explode.

"Fuck, Nora. I'm too close." Sensing she wasn't there yet, he fingered her, getting her to the edge with him.

She ate at his mouth, on fire, and he knew she was there when her body clamped around his and she moaned into his mouth, then rested her head against his shoulder, shaking.

He guided her hips up and down and soon emptied into her, the orgasm violent and crushing and so damn good he couldn't think for a while after, lost in bliss.

When he came back to himself, she was kissing him all over, her clever tongue getting him hard all over again.

"In bed this time. I want to tease you until you scream," she said.

Not one to question what the lady wanted, Deacon walked her into the back bedroom and cleaned her up, loving the small gesture that meant taking care of her was his right, and it made her happy.

"I can't wait, Nora." He lay down next to her in bed, stroking her hair, her shoulders, her breasts.

"For Christmas?" She leaned close to kiss his chest and nibbled her way to his nipple. A sexual trigger for sure. He felt a twinge of lust shoot straight from her mouth on his chest to his dick.

"For the baby," he said, finally getting it out in the open.

She paused and sat up, stunned. "Baby? What baby?"

"The one you're having in nine months." He sat up with her. "No baby?"

"Where did you get that idea?"

The rush of disappointment hit him hard. "Oh. I guess I made a mistake."

Her eyes narrowed. "You *did* read that article on my laptop." Then she glared. "Oh my God. Is all this because you thought I was pregnant?"

"Huh? All what?"

"This," she snapped. "The care and the cuddling and the lovey-dovey crap." She glanced between them, at his rising dick and her pussy. "You just came inside me."

"I asked you first." He didn't understand what he was missing.

"I thought…"

"Nora, what?" Sensing he'd messed up again without realizing how, he stopped her. Forcibly. "Nope. Not this again. We are solving this right here, right now." He left the bed and returned with the fuzzy handcuffs.

182

"Deacon?" She didn't move when he cuffed her left wrist to the bedpost. But when he cuffed the right, she suddenly came alive. "Let me go."

He left the bed and put on his boxers. Sadly, his dick hadn't yet gotten the memo they'd be postponing sex. "Relax, tiger," he said to her, wondering if she recalled that the cuffs had a button on the side for instant release. "We'll get back to sex once we have this resolved between us. This 'lovey-dovey crap' of being together is perfect. I love it." *Time to go big or go home.* "I love *you.*"

She froze. "*What?*"

"Fuck it." He started pacing. "I'm tired of keeping it in. I fucking *love you.* It scares me shitless. You're amazing and funny. You get my jokes. You think perky people are annoying. And you get sick when Mitch and Becca are so schmaltzy."

"I do." She blinked. "I'm so confused. Did you or did you not want a baby with me?"

"I didn't. I do."

"Huh?"

He swore. "Damn it. Nora, I fell for you a while ago. You're real, and you seem to understand me. But then we had that time at the cabin, and I fell all the way. Hard. I love your body, your mind, all of you. But you can be so distant, and you don't trust easily. And that makes me love you even more. I'm the same."

"Yeah." She blinked at him, still looking sexier than any woman had a right to tied up in fuzzy cuffs and naked.

"When I thought you might be pregnant with my child, it just broke anything left that could resist you. It made me see what's been there all along."

"What's that?"

"You." He kissed her, because he had to.

She kissed him back, super freaked out yet enthralled at the idea of being loved by the man she'd come to care for so deeply. But love? Did she *love* him? Truly love him? Or was it just the idea of a family with a hunky guy she'd fallen for? Hadn't Flynn seemed like her ideal husband, only to find out they'd rushed things?

"Wait. I'm confused." She tried to think. "You wanted to come inside me tonight."

"I thought you were already pregnant, and you can't get more pregnant once you already are." He shrugged. "I was confused about us using condoms this week, but I'm always fine with what you want. I just want to be with you." He paused. "But why did you let me come inside you if you weren't pregnant?"

She flushed. "Because I... Well, you made me feel so special. I felt so much for you."

"Love?"

She didn't want to say it yet. She couldn't. And she hated that he tensed when she didn't answer. "Deacon, I love being with you."

"You like my body." He nodded and put distance between them, leaning against the wall.

She felt cold. "No, not just your body. You're funny, and you're the only guy I've been with who isn't boring after ten minutes."

He seemed to thaw a little bit at that.

"I'm sorry if I'm not rushing to the altar, here," she said, feeling defensive. "But we just had unprotected sex where I could get pregnant. And the thought of a baby with you is so freaking amazing, and that weirds me out."

He smiled. "Amazing?"

184

"Something I always wanted. With the right guy."

He nodded. "Something I always wanted. With the right woman." He watched her. "So why are we not making love right now? I know you're still unsure, and I don't know why." He saw her rattle the cuff and sighed. "You know you could have removed them at any time. Fine, I'll do it." He took off both cuffs. "What's wrong, Nora? Please, be honest with me."

"I am." She sat up and patted the spot next to her. When he sat, she took his hand in hers. "Deacon, I think I might love you. But I don't know. I thought I knew before, and I've been wrong before. A lot of times. You're different. I want to be sure all these feelings I'm having are because I love you, and not that I love the *idea* of you and a baby you made more."

"Isn't that the same thing?" he asked and caressed her cheek.

She lost her train of thought. "Stop being so...so..."

"Irresistible?" he offered hopefully.

"Yes! I took a big step tonight, and I think I might have overstepped. Deacon, I could be pregnant right now."

"Yeah." He smiled. "Or not. What if we go two for two?"

"Huh?"

"You're worried about the future and unsure of us. I understand. I love you, Nora. Saying it gets easier every time I do it." He kissed her. "I also don't want to pressure you. So let me know what you want." He went to leave, and everything inside her rebelled.

She latched onto his wrist. "I'm so confused." She felt teary and hated getting weepy in front of him.

"Aw, baby. Tell you what. Let me unconfuse you." Before she could respond, he reached into the nightstand and drew out a condom. "But we'll do it the safe way, okay? Then I'll take you home. And you can think about what you want. But one way or the other, I *am* giving you a birthday present to celebrate your birthday. We're going to spend more time together, so deal with it."

God, why was he being so great? *I love you so much, Deacon.* Her heart knew what her mind didn't want to accept. Because loving Deacon this much could lead to such heartache that had repercussions. Becca was tied to his family through Mitch, and Simon totally loved the big doofus.

"We can't mess this up," she said more to herself than to Deacon.

"We won't. The only way we can is not to see what's here between us. I love you, Nora." He pulled her in for a kiss that melted her bones. "Now let me show you how much…"

CHAPTER 19

*D*eacon hadn't been able to get Sunday out of his head. Telling Nora he loved her had opened something inside him. He felt freer than he'd been in a long time. Granted, if she decided they couldn't be together for some reason, it would crush him. But he had a feeling accepting her into his life had healed that part of him that had been aching for so long.

"Well aren't you a happy camper." His father's breath puffed in the cold as more snow started to fall.

They stood in the forest beyond Mitch's house, enjoying Christmas Eve before the sun started to set. The entire family had decided to enjoy the holiday together, starting a day early, and since Nora would soon be arriving, Deacon didn't mind staying at Mitch and Becca's.

"Life is good, Dad. I'm enjoying the season."

"Uh-huh. And that's all it is?"

Deacon had danced around his mother with a vague reference to *maybe* dating Nora then disappeared before she could grill him. So she'd sicced his father on him. Smart woman.

"Dad, really? You're spying for the enemy now?"

They paused as a family of deer bounded in front of them, heading deeper into the woods.

"Huge rack on that buck," his dad murmured.

"Yeah."

"Too bad none of us are hunters."

Deacon grinned. "Mom's the only one with the stomach to kill something that gentle and beautiful for venison. I'd rather starve."

"Which is why I obey her orders, boy." His father slung an arm around his shoulders and hugged him. Hard. "Now answer the question."

"Fine." When his dad loosened his grip, Deacon relaxed. Even a few years past sixty, the old man had the strength of a grizzly. "Nora and I are dating. But we're new and keeping it quiet."

"Good for you. I like that girl. She's smart and sassy. Your mom likes her too."

"So, Dad… How did you know Mom was the right woman for you?"

His father smiled. "Ah, now, there's a question." His father dropped his arm and started walking, so Deacon did as well. "Your mother refused me four times. Took a lot of fancy footwork to get that woman to agree to a simple date. A shared malt at our favorite ice cream shop sealed the deal. That, and I could spell. Your mother's always been a stickler for good spelling."

Deacon grinned. "Must be where I get it. Nora's anal about spelling too. We play Scrabble a lot." He left out the part about the naked betting.

"Ha. We'll definitely have to play that over the next few days."

"I don't know. Nora can get pretty competitive."

"Just Nora?" His father raised a brow. "If I remember right, you and your brother got into many a fight over game night. Of course, your mother was worse."

"I remember when she put me in a headlock when I was in fourth grade. I lost at Go Fish and she made me say 'teachers are great' in four different languages."

"Yep. I sure do love that woman."

Deacon just realized something. "I guess Nora *is* a lot like Mom."

"Of course she is, or you wouldn't be in love with her, would you?"

"That's a good point, but... I mean, I never said I loved her."

His father gave him a kind smile. "Son, after the hell that Rhonda put you through, only love would get you so gone over a girl that you'd forget your parents know and see all. Yep, even when you were fighting for a moment's peace, back when Rhonda screwed you over, we knew it was bad."

Deacon blinked. "You did?"

To his shock, his father stopped walking to look into his eyes, and his dad's looked glassy. "We talked to Roy a lot, and he said you were doing better without us. It about killed us not to be by your side through your darker moments, but we didn't want to burden you. If you'd wanted our help, you'd have come to us."

"Oh, ah..." Deacon flushed. "I don't think I would have really done it. Killed myself, or anything." Deacon felt shame that his folks might think that. "I considered it. More than a few times," he admitted. "I was depressed and drinking too much."

"Oh, Son. That woman wasn't worth it." His dad put a hand on his shoulder.

"I know. But I lost football, Dad. It hurt, so much." And it still hurt, but not like it had. Deacon had other things of importance in his life now. Friends, family, love... "It just all hit me at once. But then I started to realize life existed outside sports." He chuckled. "Sounds stupid."

"Not at all. And you're still involved in sports, you knucklehead. You coach a high school football team, and you've sent how many kids to college on scholarships?"

Deacon flushed. "That's due to kid talent, not me."

"Bull. That's a good coach. That's what that is." Lee smiled. "And you let your little brother have a piece of the pie. You're a good boy, Deacon. I love you."

Deacon swallowed the ball of emotion in his throat and grinned. "I love you too, Dad." He hugged his father, who hugged him back. Though Nora had teasingly called him a clinger, he'd inherited his need for snuggling from his old man. He appreciated that his parents had always welcomed shows of emotion, though his dad really didn't like for them to see him cry.

"So, when are you and Nora going to tie the knot?" Lee asked.

"I don't know. She hasn't come around to loving me yet."

"She will. Once you're hit by a Flashman, you never recover."

"Nice, Dad."

"I still tell your mother that. Annoys the piss out of her, but I'm right." His dad walked taller on the way back to the house.

Deacon hoped Nora would realize she could trust in their relationship. He'd come to grips with his own issues, and though he would always be more suspicious than openly trusting, that he didn't fret about Nora's fidelity or integrity told him all he needed to know about her.

Now it was up to Nora to figure out what she wanted.

He could only pray it was him.

❄

NORA STARED WITH EXCITEMENT AT THE FALLING SNOW AS SHE DROVE Becca up the mountain to her house. Becca had finished with the tea shop for the holidays, and Nora had offered to drive her back home, saving Mitch a car ride.

Simon, Jenna, and a few teenage friends were having a blast of a pool party, which would end right about the time Nora and Becca arrived to celebrate Nora's birthday.

"I can't believe how excited Simon is about this holiday." Becca looked joyful, her hazel eyes bright.

"I can't believe you actually let Mitch have Ava while you went into town."

Becca frowned. "I'm not that bad."

"You have a dent in your shoulder from where your daughter's head usually lies."

Becca laughed. "Stop. I've been letting Mitch hold her too."

"Barely."

"Let's talk about you and not me," Becca said smoothly. "Have you told Deacon yet?"

"Told him what?"

"Stop it. You're a terrible liar. You know what I'm talking about."

"I'm a great liar." When Becca just gave her *the look,* Nora groaned. "I know, I know. I'm a coward."

"Yep."

"I love him, but I'm afraid if I tell him, things will change. It will be Flynn all over again."

"Flynn?"

Nora blew out a breath. "Damn it. I never was going to tell you about him."

"*What?*" Becca's eyes grew wide, so Nora focused harder on the road. "You have secrets I don't know? I tell you *everything.*"

Great. Now Becca looked hurt. Nora groaned. "Oh, stop. This is about me. Not you."

"True. Speak."

"Funny how you no longer look like I hurt your feelings, faker," Nora muttered.

"I can and will sing to the car radio. Now talk, woman."

"Fine! Flynn was a mistake I made two years ago. We were engaged for all of three weeks. I never told anyone because deep down I knew it was wrong, and I was embarrassed my nonstarter relationship went that far. I was just lonely and tired of being the odd woman out on everything."

"Oh, Nora. I'm sorry."

"You should be. I used to envy you, then I'd feel guilty about it. Neal was so perfect for you. Then you found Mitch. Talk about soulmates times two."

Becca blushed. "Yes. I never thought I could have so much in life. I've been blessed many times over." She gripped Nora's hand and squeezed. "The least of which is being given a sister, especially with the parents I have."

Nora didn't like Becca's dad and stepmother either. They lived petty little lives and had no time for their daughter or their grandson. "I agree. Your folks suck. But you're a terrific sister." Nora refused to cry.

"I am." Becca nodded. "So I can tell you when you're being foolish.

Hiding what you feel because you're afraid of being hurt is stupid. And you're too smart for that, Nora."

"Don't hold back."

"I won't. You've been alone for so long. It's not easy to find love with someone who's worthy of you. You are an awesome person. And I happen to know Deacon, and he's an awesome person. Together, you'd make an awesome couple."

Nora shrugged. "Meh. As far as a pep talk, I'd say that's on the lame side."

Becca groaned. "Yeah, I heard myself saying 'awesome' too much too. But it's true. Deacon has been through hell in his life, and he's still so supportive and sweet. Mitch and I have talked about him. Deacon's always been there for Mitch. For his family, for Roy. Heck, he's a great shoulder to lean on and would give you the shirt off his back. But he won't take help from anyone. Not Mitch, at least. Deacon really leaned on Roy a few years back, and between you and me, that hurt Mitch. But he understood. Deacon had to get himself back to a hundred percent his own way."

"Do you think he's back to a hundred percent though?"

Becca's eyes narrowed. "Before you two started dating, I would have said no. He's funny and smart, but he's always been guarded. Now he's smiling and laughing and just full of joy. It might sound corny, but it's true. And that's because of you."

"He thought I was pregnant."

"*What?*"

Thinking about the chances she'd taken made her feel really foolish. But she'd been crushing hard on Deacon, wanting a connection. "We were fooling around, not using protection, and then he saw some research I was doing for a book. About pregnancy."

"Oh my God. Why would you not use protection?"

"Hey, no judging. There were circumstances… But then the last time, I wanted him. And maybe, I don't know, I wanted his baby. Not *a* baby, *his*."

"Ah. Because you're in love with him."

"He was happy enough to contribute to the occasion," Nora said wryly. "I didn't scare him away with the possibility of kids."

"He's so great with Simon and Ava."

Nora's belly fluttered as she thought on all she admired about Deacon. "I know. He's a wonderful guy. And he can spell."

"So when are you getting married?"

WELL, DIDN'T BECCA THINK SHE WAS SO SMART. NORA GLARED AT HER cousin across the kitchen, ignoring Mitch's interest. Becca had it easy *now*. A great husband, money in the bank, and two amazing children. Nora was still reaching for her dream, to someday publish a book under her own name. She continued to strive to make ends meet, freelancing when the social media gigs went soft and doing more edits, which took time away from writing a book.

And then of course, she had to navigate a new, wonderful yet scary personal life, complete with a giant lothario who could make her orgasm with ease. How did a woman handle that? Not to mention all his exes looked like models with boobs.

Nora glanced down at herself. Well, she had the boob thing going for her. But she was nowhere as pretty as his exes. Could she trust that what she and Deacon had was real? Or was she just imprinting her own needs and feelings onto a perfectly decent—but not perfect for her—guy?

"Happy Birthday, Aunt Nora," Simon yelled across the room.

Becca appeared behind him holding a cake with a bazillion candles on it.

Deacon snorted. "Jesus, Nora. Are you turning thirty-five or fifty?"

"Jackass," she muttered.

Deacons parents, Mitch, Simon, Jenna, and a few teenagers still waiting to be picked up laughed and begged for cake.

Nora waited while everyone sang Happy Birthday to her. She focused on Deacon, who watched her with a smirk. She made her wish after blowing all thirty-five—*not fifty, Deacon*—candles.

"Oh, now your wish will come true," Jenna said, standing by Simon.

Nora shot her an evil grin.

Jenna made the sign of the cross and winced. "I'm sorry. But packing that bag for you was my way of helping."

Simon high-fived her. "Me too, Deacon."

"No problem, Simon." Deacon smiled. "I can't wait until training camp next season, can you?"

Mitch hooted. "Oh yeah. It's on. Simon, you are gonna run your ass off."

"Mitch!" Becca reprimanded, gently but firmly.

Brenda Flashman snickered.

Mitch corrected himself. "Oh, er run your *tail* off, I meant."

Deacon rolled his eyes. "Tail and ass are synonymous, Becca. Geez."

"Yeah, Becca. Geez." Nora agreed. Her cousin needed to step down a notch with her rules about cursing.

Deacon winked at her, and for some reason Nora blushed, which made him laugh.

They cut the cake, and Nora consumed a *second* slice of the decadent red velvet goodness in seconds.

Deacon ate a second as well and agreed that Becca could bake her "ass" off any day of the week.

Then Nora opened presents, to her surprise, not having expected anything but cake. Her parents had left her a few hundred dollars in cash, to spend as she liked. Deacon's parents gave her a sweater that Becca must have told them about, because it was in the right color and size. Becca bought her a pair of pricey boots Nora had had her eye on. And Mitch gave her a movie pass good for a year. After hugging and thanking everyone, she saw Simon step forward with a present.

"For you, my favorite aunt." He stepped back.

She opened up the package to find a book about forgiveness.

"You should read it a few times. It preaches *forgiving* and *forgetting*," Simon emphasized with a grin. "Oh, and I also promise to wash your car for you with a thorough detail. It's a mess."

"Thanks, you little punk." She gave him a big hug and a wet kiss he gagged over. Then she leaned in to whisper, "But I never get mad. I get even. No forgetting here, bucko." She still hadn't yet forgiven him for tricking her into meeting Becca at the tea shop.

He cringed. "I only lie for a good cause. Besides, Mom made me do it."

Her evil laugh creeped him out until Deacon clapped a hand over her mouth. "Easy, Killer. You're freaking out Simon and his friends. And me, to be honest."

The crowd dispersed as more teens went home. Mitch and Simon left to drive Jenna into town. Becca retreated to feed Ava, who had woken from her nap, and the Flashmans left Nora with Deacon, knowing smiles on their faces.

"Finally alone." He seemed nervous. "Um, come with me."

"Only if it's a good present."

"It's great."

In a lower voice as she followed him down a hall, she said, "It better not be your dick tied up with a bow."

He cracked up as he nudged her inside his bedroom, a huge guest room with an adjoined bathroom, and shut the door behind them. "That's not a bad idea. Wish I would have thought of it before I got you something else."

"Someone else's dick with a bow?"

"Stop." He was grinning when he seated them on the bed then handed her a large box, big enough to hold a small TV.

"What's in it?"

"Duh. Open it."

She did and stared, speechless.

CHAPTER 20

The laptop Nora had been drooling over, complete with all the latest tech and gadgets, as well as the software she needed, lay nestled together in the box. And it cost a small fortune.

"Deacon, this… It's too much." She kept touching the computer, in love with the sleek design and the fact he'd gotten her a red sleeve to cover it.

"I know you love red. And I'm waiting to read your love scenes. Now you have no choice but to finish the damn book."

Tears burned at the back of her eyes, and she blinked furiously as she set her presents back in the box on the floor. "You're such an ass."

He groaned. "Becca told me you'd love that. What did I do wrong?"

"Plenty! I was going to tell you I love you at Christmas. But I can't hold it in, and now it will look like you're buying my love with presents."

His wide smile was her reward for finally embracing the terrifying truth of her feelings. He chuckled. "If I'd known you were this easy, I'd have bought you a pony long before now."

She sniffed then dissolved into laughter that made her cry, but only because she found him so funny.

He caught her in a hug. "Oh man. I love you so damn much. But honey, you are one ugly crier."

"Asshole."

"Yep. There's my Nora." He kissed her forehead, waiting for her to blow her nose, and started stripping naked.

"Deacon. Now?" *Hell yeah. But I need to appear like I have some staying power, and not like I'm desperate for him all over again. Like I am all the time.*

"I want to give you one more present." Once naked, he gestured to his erection. "This, minus the bow, is for you."

She bit her lower lip. "No condom, okay?"

His smile widened. "And now your present is my present. Whatever my lady desires." He paused. "Then again, you're no lady. Whatever *my Nora* desires."

"Much better." She tore off her clothes and let him have his wicked way with her.

He had her on her back under him, on the floor because she worried the bed might squeak when they got to rocking. Sadly, Deacon moved much too slowly. By the time he'd finished playing with her breasts, she teetered on the verge of climax.

"Oh no. Not yet." He kissed her nipples, teething them while running his large hands over her breasts and belly, teasing as he inched his fingers lower, then stopping at the juncture of her thighs.

"God, fuck me already." She squirmed.

His big body kept her from moving too much. So strong, Deacon held her right where he wanted her. And she *loved* it.

"I love you," she said again, feeling out the words. They sounded right, but more, they *felt* right. "But if you don't start moving, I will kill you."

He leaned up from her breast to grin. "Now why would you do that? Then I can't fuck you as hard as you need it."

She moaned. "Do it. Please."

Deacon slowly kissed his way down her body, finally stopping at her sex. He crouched there, spreading her thighs wider so he could lie between them. "I love eating you, baby. And I'm going to make you scream, so happy birthday."

"I'll get you for this."

"Promise?" He dove in, kissing and licking her into a swirling mess.

She could only feel as he tuned her body like he owned it. She did whatever he wanted. Until finally, he blanketed her and pushed deep inside her.

"Oh yeah. So hot." He moaned. "So wet."

"*Yes, yes,*" she hissed and started coming the moment he stopped moving, fully inside her, while his pelvis brushed her sensitized clit.

Gripping him with her inner muscles, she lost herself in the ecstasy of being with the man she loved.

Deacon wasn't far behind, thrusting deep and fast and coming but not stopping.

"Oh, God." He kept pumping, and she kept climaxing.

Her orgasm seemed never-ending. She lay beneath him, quivering, as he finished, finally spent. He leaned up on his elbows and kissed her, still thick and hard inside her

Deacon rasped, "Okay, now that I've emptied on round one, it'll be safe for you to swallow on round two."

"If you can manage a round two, you're on." She groaned. "I'm exhausted. I've never come that long before."

"Because I'm the man."

She huffed, amused with him. "Oh sure. Let's make my orgasm all about you."

"Well, if we must." He withdrew and thrust back again. Little pushes while he grew harder. "Give me a little..." He kept moving, touching and caressing her.

And somehow the big bastard managed to rev her engines all over again. But this time, instead of coming inside her, he withdrew and turned around.

"A sixty-nine for your thirty-fifth. Not bad math, eh?" He didn't give her time to respond, but her mouth over him was all the answer he needed.

CHRISTMAS MORNING WAS MAGICAL. DEACON SMILED SO MUCH HIS JAW hurt, but he wouldn't have traded this time with Nora and their families for anything. He still couldn't believe the perfect woman had been there all along, and he'd been too blinded by insecurity and a lingering heartache to see it for over a year.

Everyone opened presents, and Deacon was touched to see a box of homemade cookies and a key to her cottage from Nora.

They hadn't discussed living arrangements yet, but with their explosive sexual chemistry, and just wanting to be with her all the time, he figured they'd end up moving into his house, for the sole fact he had more space.

"I love it, Nora." He kissed her in front of everyone, and the small crowd applauded.

"It's not that big a deal," Nora grumbled, then kissed him back. "Well? I guess it's okay if you clap when *I* kiss *him*."

He laughed. Becca rolled her eyes.

"Oh man. Good luck handling that one," Mitch said with a nod at Nora.

"I know, man. I know." Deacon hung his head.

Hours later, after they'd unwrapped all their gifts and enjoyed a full brunch, Deacon sat with Nora in the reading room. They sat on the couch under a blanket, facing the fire and a sleeping dog, and enjoyed the quiet.

Nora shook her head. "I'm still not sure how we went from getting Mitch and Becca together to here over a year later." She turned to look at him. "I had a major crush on you. Then you disappeared, and I half-hated you. Then, I can't explain it. It's like you were there, always hanging around. I kept running into you all over town."

"Huh. Like fate." And a great play of Roy's that had totally helped him score a winning touchdown with Nora.

"There, then not there." Nora sighed and kissed him. "I hate to admit it, but without you, my life is half empty."

"Well, I'm a glass half full kind of guy. So we'll need to be together forever to make our lives worth living." He smiled.

"Dramatic, but okay." She paused. "I love you, Deacon."

"Ah, the words. Now that is the best Christmas present a guy can get."

"Oh?" She reached into her pocket and pulled out a familiar box.

He swallowed around a dry throat. "Where did you get that?"

"From the dresser in your—I mean *our*—room. I snooped." She showed a lot of teeth. "I know I only gave you a key to my place."

"I thought it was to your heart, like, symbolic as well as a physical thing."

"Sure, sure. Let's say it was." She cleared her throat, and to his surprise, she seemed nervous. "But about this box... If it's what I think it is, then *my* gift to you includes accepting this gift *from* you."

"I'm almost confused."

"Give me the damn box," she growled.

He took it from her and left the couch to get on bended knee, his heart in his eyes, his voice thick with feeling. "Honoria Nielson, you—"

She shrieked. "I *knew* Mitch would tell you my name!"

He cleared his throat, and she quieted so he could continue. "As I was saying, Nora, you are truly a pain in my ass. And I have loved you from the moment I laid eyes on you. It just took me a lot of bad dates with boring people and some crazy hot Nora-sex to realize you're not perfect, but you're the perfect woman for me. Will you do us both the honor of agreeing to become my wife?"

Tears ran down her cheeks, and her brown eyes looked black, dark with emotion. "Best dang proposal a girl could receive. I *have* to say yes to that, or I'll look like a complete jerk." She opened the box and stared at the 2-carat, flawless, colorless, square-cut diamond ring. "Holy shit. This is worth more than everything I own! Including my new laptop."

"I had to sell a kidney, but you're worth it."

"Well, you do have a spare." She couldn't stop looking at the ring. "It's too big. It's not me."

"It's exactly you. It's beautiful and worth a lot. And you're worth more than everything to me."

"God, Deacon. I think you're the one with all the words today."

"We're playing Scrabble later—clothes on—so I'm sure to win."

"I might let you." She kissed him deeply, and he kissed her back, lost in love.

She pulled away and pushed him onto his back on the floor.

The dog had yet to move, now snoring quietly by the fire.

Nora frowned. "I hate to ask, and I know how sensitive you are about money, but damn, Deacon. How not-rich are you, anyway?"

He grinned. "Well, let's just say we'll be comfortable as long as the brewery stays in the black. But I'm hoping to someday quit my job and be a stay-at-home dad when your book career takes off. You know, to live my dream of being a kept man."

She smiled. "I'm surprisingly okay with that." Then she showed him how much she loved him, ever so slowly…

CHRISTMAS NIGHT, SIMON NODDED WITH SATISFACTION. NORA WORE one heck of a big rock on her finger. Deacon, the proud fiancé, stood by her side, hugging her close, as the new couple accepted constant congratulations from everyone, including Nora's parents over the phone.

Simon's grandparents cooed over the ring and the baby. His mom squealed and nudged Mitch every time she glanced at Nora's diamond, but Mitch only smiled and encouraged her, no sign of jealousy that his big brother might be stealing Ava's spotlight.

Jenna had mentioned that might be a possibility, but Simon had known the family would only grow tighter with his aunt and uncle now marrying.

He nodded to himself. *They should be thanking me.*

As if Deacon heard him, he locked gazes with Simon and nodded. Then he winked.

"Ha! I am the best."

"Honey, did you say something?" his mom asked as she passed by holding his sister.

Ava blinked at Simon and smiled. He'd swear she did, that it wasn't just gas.

"Nah, Mom. Just talking to myself."

"Well, we'll have to get you fitted for a new suit next year. You've already grown out of your pants from your suit for our wedding."

"Ugh."

"But on the bright side, we have another wedding to attend that I don't have to plan. Yay!"

Double ugh. Though maybe he could talk Nora and Deacon into a destination wedding. Hawaii would be awesome.

He texted Jenna, who texted him back with a lot of happy face emojis and ideas on how to make that Hawaii trip work. Man, he sure had the best girlfriend.

CHAPTER 21

One month later

$\mathcal{N}$ora finally arrived home. "I'm back."

Deacon smiled, every moment with her was brighter and better. Deacon's house now had color, plenty of books, and girl stuff without compromising his taste. She'd managed to turn his house into *their* home without too many arguments. Though he still thought he should have been able to keep that vintage girlie calendar in the downstairs den. Instead, he'd given it to Nora, who'd framed her lookalike (Ms. December) and hung the looker in the bedroom closet, which they'd then christened rather creatively.

"You did it, Deacon. You gave me the best birthday present I could ever hope for." Nora pumped her fist in the air.

"You got an agent already?" He hadn't realized she'd finished the book, though she'd been going to a few local writer meetings and had been researching how to get published while she worked on it every night, little by little, on her new laptop.

"No way. I'm not ready to query agents yet. I'm only a quarter of the way done my first draft. Slow down, tiger."

"Sure thing, killer." He sneered. She sneered back.

They laughed.

He asked, "Then what's so great about the laptop?"

She beamed. "Nothing. I'm pregnant!"

He stared, shocked. "But... But... Really?"

"It's too soon to announce it yet, but I took three tests, and they're all positive. I have a doctor's appointment scheduled for tomorrow."

He let out a yell and swung her around before realizing he should be a lot gentler. He set her down and gave her a huge kiss. "I'm so happy right now. You have no idea."

The doorbell rang, followed by the door opening and closing. Simon appeared with Mitch. As payback for Simon's favor, Simon had requested to use Deacon's SUV for practice driving. Apparently, Mitch's Porsche wasn't great in the snow. Go figure.

Simon gave him a weak smile. Mitch didn't look happy. And Deacon didn't care about any of it. Nora was going to have their baby!

Simon waved. "Um, hi, Deacon. I brought back the SUV."

Mitch sighed. "Simon..."

Simon swallowed. "Is now a good time to tell you I might have accidentally skidded into a tree with your front bumper? I swear, it's just a small smudge, no dent or anything."

"It's not that bad," Mitch agreed. "We didn't see the ice."

Nora laughed. "Today is probably the only day you could tell him and live to see tomorrow."

"Huh?" Simon stared suspiciously between them. "Are you guys drunk?"

Mitch chuckled. "High on love. Do you guys ever stop hugging?"

"You should talk," Nora said, still smiling like a loon.

Deacon grinned. "We're permanently joined," he teased. To Simon, he said, "I'm high on life, kid. But I'm suddenly in the mood for a drink."

"Great." Simon grinned. "I'll have one."

"A juice for the kid." Deacon shook his head. "Mitch? You want one?"

Mitch brightened. "Sure. You got any of that holiday ale left?"

"I do."

"I want a beer." Nora groaned. "Oh wait. Man, this is going to suck."

"Not too much, I hope." Deacon smiled. "But we have plenty of apple juice in the fridge."

Nora smiled back.

Then Deacon kissed her again and put her down with a swat to her butt.

"Not in front of the teen." But Nora was smiling as she sauntered away. "How about a round of pool? Loser does dishes. Naked."

Simon cringed. "Ew."

Deacon nodded. "And that, Nephew, is how you succeed at the quarterback sneak."

"What's that?" Nora asked over her shoulder.

"Nothing," Deacon and Simon said at the same time.

Mitch scratched his head. "You guys are weird. Now where's that beer I was promised?"

ONCE AT HOME, SIMON LET JENNA KNOW THEY'D MADE ANOTHER successful couple. Nora and Deacon showed no sign of falling out of love. Heck, they seemed gushier and more couple-like every time he saw them, which made him feel so dang good inside. Finally. The people in his life were happy and settling down.

Perhaps now Jenna would let him work on her aunt. Because if anyone needed help, it was the hot and single realtor all his friends couldn't stop talking about. Teenage boys could be gross. But even he had to admit Piper Mason was awfully pretty, even if she was a lot older than him.

Now if only Mitch and Deacon had a friend…

THANK YOU FOR READING DEACON AND NORA'S HOLIDAY ROMANCE. IF you haven't yet read Mitch and Becca's story, *Any Given Snow Day*, turn the page for a sneak peek.

HOPE'S TURN HOLIDAYS

Any Given Snow Day

NEW YORK TIMES BESTSELLING AUTHOR

MARIE HARTE

Mitch stared at a feminine version of Simon Bragg. A few inches shorter than her behemoth son, she had long, dark-brown hair, greenish-brown eyes, and a frown that would do Simon proud.

A subtle glance and he catalogued her feminine assets. Check, check, and check. A stunner if not for the scowl on her face. Her assistant, the other pretty brunette he'd seen with Simon at the game, just grinned at him before hustling away.

"Hello. Mrs. Bragg?"

"Yes?" Cool and collected.

Funny, but his heart was racing. Mitch had been with supermodels, actresses, professional athletes. Some had possessed the same qualities Rebecca Bragg did, that essence of attraction that sparked something in his brain...and in other places. But Mitch didn't do married chicks. Ever. Best to remember that.

He cleared his throat. "I'd like to talk to you about Simon."

Her frown deepened. "Is he okay? What happened?"

Mitch had debated how to broach the subject. After talking to Deacon, they'd decided Mitch should be the one to talk to her. He still wasn't sure how they'd come up with that, other than that his brother was a scum-sucking wimp who'd rather face a firing squad than an irate mother.

"As far as I know, Simon is fine. I wanted to talk to you about his attitude though."

She snorted.

Just like her son.

"And before you say this is somehow about me not understanding him because I'm the new guy, you need to know that Simon has been acting out and is pretty much annoying most of the team."

She studied him in silence.

He wondered what she saw. Did she see the regular guy who'd rather be running down a field or hiding out in his home, reading history books and watching movies? Or did she see the confident, laughing playboy everyone thought him to be?

"Come with me." She turned and walked into the back of her teahouse.

He followed her toward the sweet smells coming from a small kitchen. Entranced by the scent of vanilla and cinnamon, he took a big sniff. "What are you making?"

"Sticky buns, my version of cinnamon rolls. Hold on." She took a few steps toward the doorway and shouted, "Nora, can you watch the front? I'm in a meeting."

Nora laughed and said something he couldn't make out but apparently Rebecca could.

She flushed and returned, putting the center island between them. He wondered if her husband had a hard time dealing with her moods, then thought the lucky guy probably didn't much care. A woman who could bake and looked like her? A win-win…until she opened her mouth.

"Well?" She waited.

He just stared.

"What?"

"I'm trying to figure out how to say this without you getting offended. I would have called your husband, but Simon wouldn't give me his number."

Something that looked like pain flashed across her face. "My husband is dead. Now what did you want to talk about?"

Wow. Talk about stepping right into it. Might have been nice if the kid had explained his father was no longer alive when Mitch had mentioned the guy. "Sorry. Simon didn't tell me."

She sighed. "So what has my son done that brings the 'Amazing Flash' to my lowly shop?"

He ignored the heat on his face. "You know, if you'd heard the whole conversation, you might not be so quick to judge."

"You're here to talk about Simon?"

Fine. He wouldn't explain himself to this sexy, stuck-up viper. Wait. Where had *sexy* come from? Rebecca Bragg was more girl-next-door…with a side of sexy. Damn her full mouth.

Any Given Snow Day

ALSO BY MARIE

THE KISSING GAME

THE WORKS

Bodywork

Working Out

Wetwork

VETERANS MOVERS

The Whole Package

Smooth Moves

Handle with Care

Delivered with a Kiss

GOOD TO GO

A Major Attraction

A Major Seduction

A Major Distraction

A Major Connection

BEST REVENGE

Served Cold

Served Hot

Served Sweet

ROMANTIC SUSPENSE

POWERUP!

The Lost Locket

RetroCog

Whispered Words

Fortune's Favor

Flight of Fancy

Silver Tongue

Entranced

Killer Thoughts

WESTLAKE ENTERPRISES

To Hunt a Sainte

Storming His Heart

Love in Electric Blue

PARANORMAL

COUGAR FALLS

Rachel's Totem

In Plain Sight

Foxy Lady

Outfoxed

A Matter of Pride

Right Wolf, Right Time

By the Tail

Prey & Prejudice

ETHEREAL FOES

Dragons' Demon: A Dragon's Dream

Duncan's Descent: A Demon's Desire

Havoc & Hell: A Dragon's Prize

Dragon King: Not So Ordinary

CIRCE'S RECRUITS

Roane

Zack & Ace

Derrick

Hale

DAWN ENDEAVOR

Fallon's Flame

Hayashi's Hero

Julian's Jeopardy

Gunnar's Game

Grayson's Gamble

CIRCE'S RECRUITS 2.0

Gideon

Alex

Elijah

Carter

MARK OF LYCOS

Enemy Red

Wolf Wanted

Jericho Junction

SCIFI

THE INSTINCT

A Civilized Mating

A Barbarian Bonding

A Warrior's Claiming

TALSON TEMPTATIONS

Talon's Wait

Talson's Test

Talson's Net

Talson's Match

LIFE IN THE VRAIL

Lurin's Surrender

Thief of Mardu

Engaging Gren

Seriana Found

CREATIONS

The Perfect Creation

Creation's Control

Creating Chemistry

Caging the Beast

<u>AND MORE (believe it or not)!</u>

ABOUT THE AUTHOR

Caffeine addict, boy referee, and romance aficionado, *New York Times* and *USA Today* bestselling author Marie Harte has over 100 books published with more constantly on the way. She's a confessed bibliophile and devotee of action movies. Whether hiking in Central Oregon, biking around town, or hanging at the local tea shop, she's constantly plotting to give everyone a happily ever after. Visit http://marieharte.com and fall in love.

And don't forget to subscribe to Marie's Newsletter via her website.

NEWSLETTER

facebook.com/marieharteauthorpage

twitter.com/MHarte_Author

goodreads.com/Marie_Harte

bookbub.com/authors/marie-harte

instagram.com/marieharteauthor

CPSIA information can be obtained
at www.ICGtesting.com
Printed in the USA
LVHW112148230921
698625LV00014B/166